ROBERT B.
PARKER'S
FOOL ME
TWICE

NOVELS BY ROBERT B. PARKER

By MICHAEL BRANDMAN

ROBERT B.
PARKER'S
FOOL ME
TWICE

A JESSE STONE MYSTERY

First published in Great Britain in 2013 by

Quercus
55 Baker Street
7th Floor, South Block
London
W1U 8EW

A CIP catalogue record for this book is available
from the British Library

ISBN 978 1 78206 476 3 (HB)
ISBN 978 1 78206 477 0 (TPB)
ISBN 978 1 78206 478 7 (EBOOK)

10 9 8 7 6 5 4 3 2 1

Typeset by Ellipsis Digital Limited, Glasgow

Printed and bound in Great Britain by Clays Ltd, St Ives plc

For Joanna,
who makes the world go round . . .
and for Joan and Bob

Fool me once, shame on you.

Fool me twice, shame on me.

1

Jesse Stone's cruiser pulled up to the stop sign on Paradise Road, preparing to make a right turn onto Country Club Way.

A warm fall breeze blew gently through the cruiser's open windows. The red and yellow leaves of the elms and maples fluttered haphazardly in the wind. Jesse raised his face to the early-morning sun.

He noticed the car on his left, a late-model Audi A5 coupe, come to a complete stop beside him.

When the driver looked in his direction, Jesse nodded to him.

The Audi pulled away and proceeded through the intersection.

A Mercedes sedan barreled through the stop sign and

broadsided the Audi. The Mercedes was doing at least fifty in a twenty-five-mile-per-hour zone.

The Audi collapsed into itself. The impact punched it off the road and into a ditch, where it bounced precariously a couple of times before sliding to an upright stop.

The alarm systems on both cars began to shriek. Front and side air bags deployed in a vicious rush of compressed air, pinning both drivers to their seats.

The Mercedes was driven by a young female. Jesse had seen her looking down as she ran the stop sign. She must have been texting.

He grabbed his cell phone and called the station.

Molly Crane answered.

"I've got a bad one at the corner of Paradise and Country Club. Send the entire sideshow. Ambulance. CSI unit. Hazmat team. Also Suitcase."

"I'm on it, Jesse."

"Oh, and call Carter Hansen, will you? Tell him I'll be late."

Jesse switched on the flashing light bar on top of his cruiser and inched closer to the accident. He stopped in front of the Audi, got out, and walked over to it.

The driver had been immobilized by the deployed air bags. He was sandwiched tightly between his seat and the bag.

He was middle-aged and overweight, wearing a navy blue sport jacket, a button-down white dress shirt, and a gray-and-pink polka-dot bow tie. A chevron-style mustache concealed his upper lip. He was unconscious.

Jesse called out to him.

"Can you hear me, sir?"

There was no response.

Jesse pulled open the door. He reached inside, disabled the alarm system, and used his Leatherman to deflate the air bags.

The man slumped back in his seat. Blood seeped from his nose.

Jesse checked for a pulse.

At least the guy was alive.

Jesse turned and stepped over to the Mercedes.

The teenage driver had also been pinned by the air bags. She wore a uniform bearing the insignia of one of Paradise's best private schools. Unlike the other driver, she was awake and alert.

"Are you hurt," Jesse said.

"I don't think so," she said.

Jesse nodded.

"Just get me out of this fucking car," she said.

Jesse looked at her. Satisfied that she wasn't injured, he circled the Mercedes, checking for damage. Despite the intensity of the crash, the car was relatively intact. He opened the passenger-side door and spotted the item he was looking for.

He walked back to the cruiser, retrieved an evidence bag, then returned to the Mercedes. Slipping a rubber glove on his right hand, he reached beneath the still-inflated air bag and grabbed the iPhone from the car floor.

"What are you doing," the girl said. "Why aren't you getting me out of here?"

Jesse ignored her.

He bagged the phone and put it inside his cruiser.

When he returned to the Mercedes, the girl was attempting to wriggle her way out of it.

"Be easier if I deflate the air bags," Jesse said.

"Then what are you waiting for," she said.

Jesse poked the air bags with his Leatherman. He also disabled the alarm system. The quiet was a blessing.

Now freed, the young woman opened her door and started to get out.

Jesse pushed the door closed.

"Stay where you are until the medics arrive."

"Don't tell me what to do," she said, struggling to open the door.

"I'm instructing you not to get out of the car until you're seen by a medic."

"I'm totally fine. Even a moron can see that."

Jesse looked at her.

He removed a pair of handcuffs from his service belt. He grabbed the girl's left wrist and cuffed it to the steering wheel.

He heard sirens in the distance.

"What do you think you're doing," she said.

"You do know it's illegal to text while driving?"

The girl didn't respond.

"There's an injured man in the car that you hit."

"It was an accident."

"Caused by you."

"Have you any idea who I am?"

"Have you no concern for the other driver?"

"Yeah, sure. Of course. Courtney Cassidy."

"What?"

"I'm Courtney Cassidy."

"Nicely alliterative."

"What?"

Jesse remained silent.

"My father is Richard Cassidy."

The sirens grew closer.

"I want my phone," she said.

"It's been placed into evidence."

"What do you mean it's been placed into evidence?"

"I confiscated it."

"I want to speak to my father."

"You can make a phone call when you get to the police station."

"I'm not going to the police station."

Jesse looked at her for a few moments. Then he walked away.

"Hey," she called after him.

He ignored her.

She called again.

"Hey, dickwad," she said.

Another police cruiser and an ambulance appeared on Paradise Road, sirens blaring, lights flashing. They pulled to a stop near Courtney's Mercedes.

Suitcase Simpson emerged from the cruiser. He spotted Jesse and walked toward him.

Two EMTs got out of the ambulance. Jesse pointed them to the Audi.

"What happened," Suitcase said.

"Girl was texting. She ran the stop sign and hit the Audi."

Suitcase looked over at her.

"Why is she cuffed to the steering wheel?"

"Disobedience."

"Okay."

"If the medics clear her, you can arrest her."

"Charges?"

"Reckless endangerment. Running a stop sign. Texting while driving. Resisting arrest. Arrogance."

"I don't think arrogance is a chargeable offense, Jesse," Suitcase said.

"Okay. Forget arrogance. Make a big deal out of reading her her rights, though. Do it slowly and deliberately."

"Why?"

"Because I don't like her," Jesse said.

The medics were now at the Mercedes, evaluating Courtney. One of them stepped away and spoke to Jesse and Suitcase.

"Guy's floating in and out of it," he said. "Looks like he suffered some head trauma. We'll take him to Paradise General."

"The girl," Jesse said.

"She seems okay," the medic said. "If you're going to have an accident, probably best it be in a Mercedes."

"You taking her to the hospital, too," Suitcase said.

"We're not quite finished examining her, but it doesn't appear necessary. Is there anyone who can remove the handcuffs, by the way?"

Jesse handed the key to Suitcase.

"Cell phones," Jesse said with a snort. "Big-time dangerous. There need to be more serious consequences for using them while driving. The current laws are a joke."

After her handcuffs were removed, Courtney got out of the damaged Mercedes and headed in Jesse's direction.

She might one day be pretty, Jesse thought, but today wasn't that day. Her flat-ironed yellow hair hung limply around her plain round face, still plump with the last vestiges of baby fat. Her makeup was heavy and inexpertly applied. Her green plaid uniform was as flattering as a prison jumpsuit. Her pale blue eyes, however, flashed defiance.

"Will one of you call my parents. I want to go home," she said.

"No, ma'am," Jesse said.

She moved closer to him.

"I said I want to go home."

"You're under arrest," Jesse said. "You're going to jail."

"Arrest?"

"Correct."

"You can't arrest me. I'm Courtney Cassidy."

Jesse looked at her.

Then he turned to Suitcase and said, "Book her, Danno."

2

The insistent ringing of the doorbell at her Beverly Hills estate finally caught Marisol Hinton's attention.

She struggled to stand. Once she was on her feet, she was reminded of the pain all over again.

She peered through the peephole. Standing outside was her agent, Sarah Fine.

Sarah was a severe-looking woman engaged in a losing battle with her weight. A loose-fitting black Armani suit worn over a gray silk blouse barely camouflaged her problem. The five-hundred-dollar José Eber haircut helped only a little.

"I'm not really up for company," Marisol said, loudly enough for Sarah to hear.

"I'll keep ringing until you let me in," Sarah said.

After a while, Marisol sighed, unlocked the door, and stepped aside so that Sarah could enter. Then she closed the door and locked it.

Marisol Hinton was currently one of Hollywood's flavor-of-the-month starlets. She was an adroit comedienne, still a beauty at age twenty-seven, and sexy enough to hold the screen opposite the rash of young leading men who were themselves vying for stardom.

"Let me look at you," Sarah said.

Marisol shied away, hiding her face.

"Show me," Sarah said.

She turned her face to Sarah.

Her left eye was deeply discolored and swollen shut. There was a cut on her left cheek, the result of his ring having raked her face when he hit her.

"My God," Sarah said. "You have to do something."

"I changed the locks. I heightened the security watch."

"That's not enough. You have to call the police."

Marisol shrugged.

Her mansion was located in the storied Holmby Hills neighborhood of Beverly Hills. It had once been owned by Groucho Marx, and in its heyday, the gated estate played host to the cream of old Hollywood. It boasted a kidney-shaped swimming pool with a grotto, a Pancho Segura–designed tennis court, a koi pond, which often fell victim to marauding raccoons, and a screening room that Groucho himself had designed, with comfortable seating for twenty.

"You've seen the doctor," Sarah said.

"Not much he could do."

Sarah reached out and took Marisol in her arms.

"Please let me help you," she said. "The agency has a very long reach in this town."

"I'm a big girl. I should have known better." She sighed.

"I thought he'd be a star," she said. "I had visions of us as the new power couple."

Sarah released her and stepped back.

"You've gotten an offer," Sarah said. "Picture called *A Taste of Arsenic*."

Marisol looked at Sarah.

"Starts filming in four weeks. Eliza Morgan is pregnant and had to withdraw. They want you."

"Four weeks," Marisol said.

She touched her face.

"What hasn't healed we'll fix with makeup," Sarah said.

"Can I read it?"

Sarah reached into her bag and handed her the screenplay.

"They need to know today."

"I'll read it now."

"It shoots on the East Coast. A perfect opportunity to get away from him."

"Where?"

"Small town in Massachusetts."

"Which one?"

"I doubt you've heard of it. A place called Paradise."

3

Jesse pulled his cruiser into the circular driveway of the Paradise Country Club and parked in front.

The red-brick clubhouse was one of the architectural grande dames of Paradise. Constructed in the 1920s, it was colonial in style, ostentatious in appearance, and currently exhibiting multiple signs of disrepair. The average age of the membership was sixty-plus, and rumor had it that enrollment was faltering.

He entered the clubhouse and headed toward the dining room at the back of the building, the floor-to-ceiling windows of which offered excellent views of the first tee of the Robert Trent Jones–designed golf course, as well as the Olympic-size swimming pool, which was currently being drained in anticipation of encroaching winter.

The room was nearly empty as Jesse crossed it and approached Carter Hansen's table.

Seated with Hansen was selectman Morris Comden, as well as Frances "Frankie" Greenberg, the line producer of the upcoming feature motion picture *A Taste of Arsenic*, which was soon to start filming in Paradise.

"Sorry I'm late," Jesse said as he sat down.

"We were beginning to give up hope," Carter Hansen said.

Jesse smiled weakly.

"Ms. Greenberg was just explaining the intricacies of filmmaking," Hansen said. "It all sounds very exciting."

Frankie Greenberg was in her mid-thirties, sharply attractive and radiating confidence. She wore a midnight-blue Stella McCartney stretch-cotton bomber jacket, a diamond-print silk blouse, and a pair of slim-cut jeans and open-toed Jimmy Choo sandals. Her jet-black hair was cut boyishly short, in style with the current Hollywood trend. Her dark green eyes sparkled with intelligence.

"Actually," she said, "it's not all that exciting."

"Why not," Hansen said.

"Why isn't it exciting?"

"Yes."

"Line producing a movie is the equivalent of running a mid-sized company," Frankie said.

Jesse took a sip of coffee and leaned back in his chair.

"For instance," Frankie said, "I'm in charge of running the business of the movie here on location. Long hours. Lots of stress. The studio production manager watches me like a hawk. Exciting? Not exactly. It's exciting for the executive wonks back in Hollywood, though. They get to shmooze up the creative team . . . the writers, the director, the department heads. They also get to do all of the casting."

"And you," Comden said.

"I get to hire the grunts."

"The grunts," Hansen said.

"Distant locations are frequently chosen because of the tax advantages they offer. Millions of dollars are often rebated back to the production company by cities and states eager to have their business. Like here. The only caveat is that the rebates are dependent on the movie hiring local workers."

"The grunts," Hansen said.

"Yes."

"You mean the more locals you hire, the greater the cash rebates," Comden said.

"Yes," Frankie said.

"And you get to hire them," Hansen said.

"And manage them, too. I also get to devise the shooting schedule and then supervise it. I monitor each day's progress according to that schedule, and God help us if we fall behind."

"How could you fall behind," Hansen said.

"That's exactly what the bigwigs in Hollywood ask."

"And how do you answer them?"

"If we fall behind?"

"Yes."

"I blame everything on the director."

Jesse smiled.

"Actually, it's all in the anticipation," Frankie said. "It's my job to know how we're faring as each day progresses. If we fall even fifteen minutes behind schedule, I know it and I pounce."

"On who?"

"On them all. Like a ton of bricks. I threaten them. I threaten to fire them. I've even been known to threaten their lives."

"A nice girl like you," Comden said.

"Nice is illusory," she said.

"Meaning?"

"I'm lethal," she said.

Jesse grinned.

They all sipped their coffee in silence.

"Who did you say was going to star in *A Touch of Arsenic*," Comden said at last.

"Marisol Hinton," Frankie said.

"She's a wonderful actress," Hansen said.

"Beautiful, too," Comden said.

Frankie didn't say anything.

"Most of your communication regarding Paradise will involve Chief Stone here," Hansen said.

Frankie turned her attention to Jesse.

"Chief Stone," she said.

"Jesse."

"Nice to meet you, Jesse. I'm afraid we're going to shoot up your town."

"We promise not to shoot back," he said.

"Chief Stone is known for his trenchant wit," Hansen said.

"Then I'm sure we'll get along fine," Frankie said.

The breakfast wound down. The two selectmen finished their coffee and stood. After Comden shook Frankie's hand and Hansen gave her an awkward hug, they said their good-byes.

Frankie lingered for a few moments. As did Jesse.

"You think making movies is hard," she said. "Next to a breakfast like this, it's a cakewalk."

Jesse smiled.

"He doesn't like you, does he," Frankie said.

"It's that obvious?"

"Let's just say you aren't cut from the same cloth."

Jesse didn't respond.

"We're going to be a pain in the ass, you know."

"I do know."

"May I apologize in advance?"

"No apology necessary. Actually, I'm looking forward to it."

"Tell me that again in week three."

Jesse smiled.

"Are you a native or an import," she said.

"Import."

"From?"

"L.A."

"Really?"

"Angeleno born and bred."

"Really?"

"LAPD veteran, too."

"Really?"

"Are your conversational skills always this limited," he said.

"No. Uh, no. Forgive me. You surprised me," she said.

"Because I'm from L.A.?"

"I had no idea. Me, too."

"From L.A.?"

"Burbank. My father was an accountant at Warner's."

"Family business," Jesse said.

"Once bitten," she said.

Jesse smiled.

"How did you wind up here," she said.

"Long story."

Frankie didn't say anything.

"Would take an entire dinner to tell it properly," Jesse said.

"Are you suggesting we have dinner?"

"I am."

She looked at him.

"Okay," she said.

He looked at her.

"Goody," he said.

4

Ryan Rooney remembered the first time.

He had been cast in a hastily assembled potboiler called *Tomorrow We Love,* which was filming in Santa Fe, New Mexico, starring Marisol Hinton. Ryan was playing a small-town schoolteacher with whom she fell in love after he had improbably managed to save her life.

Truth was, he hated the script, and under different circumstances would have passed on it. But the chance to be seen opposite Marisol Hinton outweighed the movie's many shortcomings.

Ryan was closing in on thirty. Although the Hollywood consensus was that he had promise, he had yet to score a breakthrough.

He had tirelessly worked the system and was usually considered for most of the big roles in his age range. But now he was starting to compete with the next generation of wannabes, and he was fearful of slipping farther down the ladder.

So he accepted the role. He had no idea how much he would come to regret it.

The shooting of *Tomorrow We Love* was hampered by bad weather, resulting in numerous delays. Spirits were damp. Tempers were short.

There was tension between Ryan and the director, an inexperienced wunderkind who had caught the brass ring with a short film he wrote and directed that had been nominated for an Oscar. Their volatile disagreements made the set toxic.

But the production delays had encouraged a kind of friendship between Ryan and his personal driver, Bruce Stewart. On one of Ryan's Saturdays off, Stewart promised him a mind-blowing experience, and visited Ryan's hotel room with a stash of Shabu, the latest incarnation of the designer drug crystal meth.

Ryan was generally wary of taking drugs. He was afraid they might negatively impact his work. But the tension on the set had made him depressed and cranky, so he paid close attention when Stewart showed him how to fire up the Shabu.

At first Ryan felt nothing. He took another toke, and when it finally hit his system, it rocked him. He had never before experienced anything like it.

After Stewart left the hotel room, Ryan was alone. He became aware that the drug was producing in him euphoria unlike any he had ever known.

He was mostly an unhappy person, and he had been since childhood. Generally, he was angry and insecure, guarded and secretive. He was normally on edge and anxious.

But the drug relaxed him. He began to feel loose and easy. And he felt omnipotent. For some odd reason, a goofy grin lit up his face.

His mind was racing. He believed that nothing was beyond his reach. He felt emboldened in a way he could never have imagined. And he was unbelievably horny. He had a desperate need to get laid.

Marisol Hinton flitted across his mind, but he quickly dismissed the idea as too far-fetched. She was the star, after all. He considered his makeup person, then the script supervisor. Finally, the second assistant director came to mind. He rejected them all. He felt it would be unseemly for him to be banging members of the crew.

He thought again of Marisol. She had been nice to him. Flirty, even. On top of everything else, she was drop-dead gorgeous. And he was feeling so, so good.

They were staying at the same hotel. On the same floor, to be exact. He knew she was there alone. When they first met, she mentioned that she had been single for a while.

Ryan made his decision.

What the hell.

He wandered down the hall and knocked on her door.

"Who is it," Marisol said.

"It's Ryan."

"Ryan?"

"Ryan Rooney."

She opened the door.

She stood there, wrapped in a loosely tied hotel bathrobe. Her rich auburn hair cascaded around her neck and shoulders in wispy curls. She smelled of musk. Her eyes were wide, her expression open yet knowing.

"This is a surprise," she said.

"May I come in?"

"Sure," she said, standing back to allow him to enter. "What brings you to my door on such a gloomy day?"

"I don't know. You were on my mind."

"I was?"

He couldn't stop looking at her mouth.

"Yes."

"In what way?"

He suddenly took her in his arms and kissed her.

Surprised, she pulled away from him.

"What's gotten into you, Ryan," she said.

He stared at her, his intentions barely concealed.

She moved farther away.

"This is so unexpected," she said. "Perhaps it's not such a good idea, your being here. After all, we are working together."

"We're playing lovers," he said.

"That's just it," she said. "We're playing lovers."

"I like playing your lover."

He stepped closer and kissed her again.

She stepped back again.

"Maybe I'm not making myself clear," she said.

"Maybe I'm not making myself clear," Ryan said, closing in on her.

He touched her hair. He took a handful of it and pressed it to his nose and lips.

"You smell wonderful," he said.

She didn't say anything.

He gently slid his hand along her cheek, stopping at her lips, which he traced with his fingertips.

She sighed.

He moved his hand down her neck. He lowered his head and brushed his lips against it.

She didn't stop him.

He untied her bathrobe and reached inside. She shuddered.

He removed the robe, put his arms around her, and pulled her into him. He kissed her again, softly at first, then with more urgency. His hands roamed her back.

She leaned away for a moment and looked in his eyes.

Then she took his hand and led him into her bedroom.

By the time he returned to his own room early the next morning, they were bound to each other.

5

When Jesse arrived at the station, he found reporters from the *Paradise Daily News* and the local TV station already camped out in front. They shouted questions at him as he walked by.

Jesse called to Molly as he headed for his office.

"Would you be so kind as to join me," he said.

"You forgot the 'Good morning' part," she said.

She stood up and followed him inside.

He was already seated at his desk, thumbing through his phone messages.

"Courtney Cassidy," he said.

"You got that right," Molly said. "Seems you busted Paradise's most notable debutante."

Jesse didn't say anything.

"The DA's office called. Marty Reagan is anxious to speak with you."

"She's been put in a cell?"

"And relishing every minute of it, too. For the last half-hour she's been hollering, 'Police brutality.'"

Jesse selected one of the messages, picked up the phone, and dialed the number.

"Jesse Stone for Mr. Reagan," he said.

Marty Reagan picked up the call.

"What in hell have you done," Reagan said.

"Who, me?"

"Yes, you. I've gotten calls from half the lawyers at Cone, Oakes. I gather she's in custody."

"'She' being . . . ?"

"Don't fuck around, Jesse. The Cassidys are out for bear."

"She ran a stop sign and nearly totaled two vehicles. She was texting at the time."

"And that's why you arrested her?"

"She did manage to break a few laws."

"Her old man's Richard Cassidy."

"I don't care if he's Hopalong Cassidy. The driver of the car she hit still hasn't regained consciousness."

"So what do you suggest I do?"

"Make her the poster girl for a 'No Texting While Driving' campaign."

"Which means?"

"Charge her to the full extent of the law. Alert the media. Request jail time and a hefty fine. Stir the pot. Seek the death penalty. You know, the usual."

"You mean the usual for people you don't particularly like."

"Listen, Marty, we don't even know whether the other driver is gonna survive. Things could turn out a whole lot worse for her if he doesn't."

"Don't exaggerate. In the meantime, the girl's seventeen. No priors. And she's exceptionally well connected. Plus, I'm hearing that the guy's condition isn't that serious."

"So?"

"So none of this is going to fly, Jesse. Richard Cassidy has enormous influence in this town."

"You mean he throws his money around?"

"That, too. She'll be out in less than an hour."

Jesse sighed.

"Do the best you can, Marty," he said.

"Don't hold your breath on this one, Jesse. Arraignment's at noon."

"Fast."

"Money talks."

"You need me there?"

"You'd only make things worse."

"Gee, thanks," Jesse said.

"I'll call you," Reagan said.

6

S arah Fine's office," the voice on the other end of the line
said.

"Hi, Karen. It's Marisol."

"Hi, Ms. Hinton. Let me see if I have her."

After several seconds, Karen came back on the line.

"You're on with Sarah," she said.

"Hi, honey," Sarah said.

"I'll do it," Marisol said.

"I knew you would."

"It's a good script."

"Eric's still working on it. He's doing a dialogue pass especially for you."

"I was going to ask about that."

"He's already ahead of you. Oh, and they're shooting digital."

"Digital?"

"Not on film."

"I hate digital. It makes everything look like the evening news."

"It's the new standard, however."

"Yes, but how will it make me look?"

"Mahvelous, dahling. You'll look mahvelous."

"I'm not kidding, Sarah. I hear nightmare tales about digital. Mary Beth George walked off a Disney project because she thought she looked old and wrinkled."

"Leo Stribling is shooting it."

"Leo? I love Leo."

"Leo loves you. He'll make you look sensational."

"I hope so, Sarah. Don't forget I've got these fucking bruises on my face."

Sarah didn't say anything.

"I blame myself. I should have thrown him out sooner."

"Try not to torture yourself. It's not your fault."

Marisol didn't say anything.

"I'm thrilled that you like the script," Sarah said.

"What about the revisions?"

"What about them?"

"I have lots of ideas."

"I'm sure you do, honey. But for now, I'd leave Eric alone if I were you."

"But I hope he's open to my thoughts."

"I think you should keep your thoughts to yourself. We've been down that road before."

"I don't know . . ."

"Marisol, listen to me. I'm your agent and your friend. The last time you worked for Eric, there was friction. This time, leave it alone. Don't piss anyone off."

Marisol didn't say anything.

"I mean it."

"Okay, okay."

"Get some sun. Get some rest. I'll holler when they're ready for fittings."

"Maybe they'll want to see some of my own clothes."

"Let them decide that. Be a good soldier, Marisol. This is an important job for you. You need it. Keep that in mind."

"So what you're saying is, 'Shut the fuck up.'"

"That's exactly what I'm saying."

7

Jesse was sitting in his office, drinking coffee.

Molly walked in and planted herself in the visitor's chair opposite his desk.

"So how obnoxious was Carter Hansen about this movie business," she said.

"He was on his best behavior."

"He get all gooey about Marisol Hinton?"

"Like she was Angelina Jolie."

"This movie business will drive us all crazy, you know."

"I know."

"I'm hoping it doesn't make me nuts."

"I'll keep on the lookout for any telltale signs."

He grinned at her.

"Well, wasn't this conversation a big waste of my time," Molly said as she stood. "You had a call from Belva Radford, by the way."

"What could she possibly want?"

"She wouldn't tell me."

"She'll keep me on the phone for an hour."

"You got something better to do?"

Molly stood, stretched, and left the office.

Jesse called after her, "What's her number?"

"You could look it up," she said.

Jesse dialed the number. An ancient spinster and a local busybody, Belva Radford believed it her birthright to bring her every complaint directly to the chief of police. She had done it to Tom Carson, Jesse's predecessor, and now it was Jesse's turn.

"How can I help you today, Belva," Jesse said, holding the phone slightly away from his ear.

"Has there been some sort of increase in the Paradise utility rates," she said.

"Not that I'm aware of."

"Well, my water bill's higher."

"Are you using more water?"

"No."

"How do you know it's higher?"

"Every month I write down what I pay Paradise Water and

Power, and every month I compare it to what I paid them a year ago."

"That's very efficient, Belva."

"Don't condescend to me, young man. Just 'cause I'm old doesn't mean I need to have my cheeks tweaked by the chief of police."

Jesse didn't say anything.

"Don't go all quiet on me, Jesse."

"I'm sorry, Belva. I wasn't aware I was being condescending."

"Then pay closer attention. In any event, my water bills for the months of August and September were higher than they were a year ago."

"And you're certain you weren't using more water?"

"I checked the meter readings."

"And?"

"They were the same as they were a year ago."

"But it cost you more?"

"Yes."

"Did you receive a notification of a rate increase?"

"No. Did you?"

"Not that I'm aware of," he said.

"So what are you going to do about it," she said.

"Let me ask around."

"About other people's water bills?"

"Yes."

"Okay. But I don't want you shunting me aside 'cause I'm old. I want answers."

"If you'll let me get off the phone, I'll try to get you some."

"Don't be fresh, Jesse."

"I'll get back to you, Belva."

"I'll be waiting," she said, and hung up the phone.

Jesse put down the receiver and stared out the window for a while.

Paradise is a small town, he thought.

Then he called out to Molly, who was leaning in the doorway, one hand on her hip.

"What?"

"Are you aware of any recent increases in W and P water rates?"

"Why?"

"Belva Radford says her bills are higher."

"Belva Radford's a head case."

"That may be so, but she's still entitled to an answer."

"Then you'll have to give her one."

"I'm aware of that. That's why I'm asking you. Could you call over to W and P and ask whether there have been any recent rate hikes?"

"I'll have to check my schedule," she said.

"Quit giving me a hard time, Molly. Just call and find out, will you, please?"

"I'll take it under advisement."

Then she walked back to her desk.

Jesse watched her.

This is going to be a long day, he thought.

8

After a rash of disappointing meetings with a handful of assistant casting directors, Ryan returned to the mansion he shared with Marisol.

Things had slowed considerably for him, and he thought that if he could at least get the assistants talking about him, perhaps they might be more successful in finding him work. But it was fruitless. Although it remained unspoken, Ryan was aware that people knew he and Marisol were having issues and they wanted to wait until things resolved themselves before they risked antagonizing her by casting him.

He parked the Prius in front, picked up his shoulder bag, and headed for the house.

When he put his key in the lock, it didn't fit. He looked at it to make certain it was the right key. It was. He tried it again, but it still didn't fit.

He walked around to the back of the house and tried to unlock the kitchen door. That key didn't work, either.

He then tried every other door of the mansion, but his keys worked in none of them.

"She changed the locks," he said to himself.

Which pissed him off. He rang the bell. He banged on the door. There was no response.

He considered breaking a window, but he knew that the glass was reinforced and all he would succeed in doing would be to attract the attention of the security service.

Things had gone badly for him since he married her. He knew she was a bigger star than he, but his expectations were that his star would rise, not fall, as a result of their marriage. He hadn't been prepared for the level of attention she received wherever they went. And the manner in which she diminished him.

In the paparazzi photos, he was always in the near background, standing slightly to her left, an insincere smile plastered on his face.

She often neglected to introduce him to the important people at the Hollywood functions they frequently attended. When his agency dumped him because they didn't want to represent "Mr. Marisol Hinton," he became alarmed.

He tried to talk it over with her.

"I'm hurting here," he'd said, on their way home from a party honoring Tom Hanks.

"'Hurting,'" she said.

"Nothing's going right. I wish there was something you could do to help me."

"Like what," she said icily.

"I don't know, Marisol. We were doing so well for a while. Now I get the feeling you'd be happier alone."

She didn't say anything.

"Would you?"

"Would I what?"

"Be happier without me."

"Don't start, Ryan."

"'Start'? You could make a big difference for me. If you tried."

"You could make a difference for yourself if you stopped with the crystal meth."

"I don't ever use it when I'm working."

"That's a load of crap, Ryan, and you know it."

"Do you still care about me?"

"About you or your career?"

"About me."

"Of course I care about you. I had such hopes for you. For us."

"Then help me, Marisol. Make an effort on my behalf. Let people know that you think I'm a talent. If you'll at least do that, I'll stop using."

She looked at him.

"All right," she said.

Then, a couple of weeks later, at a benefit dinner for the Motion Picture & Television Country House and Hospital,

Marisol engaged in an intimate conversation with George Cloo-
ney and left Ryan standing alone, in his brand-new Versace tux-
edo, ignored. He was livid.

If she had really wanted him to succeed, he reasoned, she
would have insisted that her big-time talent agency represent
him, which would have been tantamount to an industry-wide
show of her support for him. When that didn't happen, the
town, fickle and fearful as it was, backed away from him.

He stewed. He used greater amounts of the methamphet-
amine. Things became worse between them.

One night, after a party at Charlize Theron's house, at which
he drank too much, Ryan raped Marisol. Afterward, she lay in
their bed, crying. Realizing what he had done, he apologized
profusely. He begged her for forgiveness.

Things got briefly better. Then they got worse.

One night he smacked her. And raped her again. Which soon
became a pattern.

And now she had locked him out.

When he noticed the Beverly Hills Safe Homes patrol car
pull to a stop in front of the house and saw two armed guards
emerge, he realized that reconciliation wasn't in the cards. He
got into his Prius and drove away.

Whenever a movie is filmed in a small town, it's the equivalent of an invasion of that town by a large army.

First come the production vehicles, led by a convoy of dozens of oversized trucks. Then come the motor homes for on-set use by cast and key staff, specially constructed mobile dressing rooms, fully outfitted bathrooms on wheels, catering vans, picture cars that will actually appear in the movie, special vehicles for use by the stars, and a multitude of additional personal vehicles.

A great many people involved in the making of a movie are imported, meaning that a huge number of production personnel suddenly show up on location, all in need of housing. They gobble up every available hotel and motel room. In many cases, even space in private homes is secured for them.

The logistics of moving the personnel and all the vehicles from one location to another every day are staggering. Their impact on the life of an unsuspecting community can be devastating.

The invasion of Paradise had begun in earnest. What had just yesterday been a lazy summer resort town had quickly morphed into a noisy, crowded, traffic-beleaguered nightmare.

A large section of the Paradise Car Park had been rented to the movie company for use as a permanent base camp, resulting in a downtown parking logjam.

Traffic was disrupted. Cars were frequently held up during the shooting, forced to wait endlessly until a shot was completed and the traffic could then be released. In some instances, entire streets involved in the filming were closed. Nobody knew what might be in store for them each time they turned a corner.

In the evenings, movie people swarmed the town restaurants, often preempting the locals. They invaded the taverns and the bars, frequently disturbing the quiet of a neighborhood with their loud and boisterous behavior.

Carter Hansen couldn't have been happier, however. His days had new purpose. He circulated through town, preening, puffing himself up, introducing himself to the movie people as the head selectman. He was overjoyed by the money that the movie personnel poured into the Paradise cash registers.

Jesse had appointed Suitcase Simpson to serve as the liaison between the movie company and the police department.

"I've never been a liaison before," Suitcase said to Jesse as they ate breakfast at Daisy's. Suitcase was working on an oversized breakfast burrito. Jesse was halfway through a cheese Danish. A pot of coffee stood in front of them.

"There's a first time for everything," Jesse said.

"These movie people are very demanding."

"Stand tall."

"Don't trivialize this, Jesse. I'm already weathering a shit storm."

"Then you're gonna want to be wearing boots."

"That's not very supportive."

"Nonsense. I have every confidence in you."

"I don't really know what I'm doing."

"You'll learn as you go."

"I wish I was as sure of that as you are."

"Let me share a bit of movie lore with you," Jesse said, as he leaned closer to Suitcase and lowered his voice.

"There was once a great Hollywood producer called Joseph E. Levine. He made *The Graduate*. The story goes that his assessment of the movie business was, 'If it were so difficult, those that do, couldn't.' Keep that in mind, Suit. You won't be dealing with brain surgeons here."

"How do you know this stuff?"

"I used to live in L.A."

"So what are you saying?"

"I'm saying that however many movie meetings you may be forced to attend, more than likely you'll be the smartest person in the room."

Jesse and Frankie were in the taproom at The Gray Gull, away from the din of the crowded dining room. Strings of glimmering mini-lights that were hung above the bar cast a glow that bounced off the oversized mirror behind it, enhancing the room's muted lighting. The faint tinkling of a piano could be heard in the background.

Frankie was picking at her crab cakes and sipping a California Cabernet. Jesse sliced into his medium-rare porterhouse, his second Carlsberg lager at his elbow.

"So you know more than you let on," she said.

"Can't be avoided when you're a cop in L.A.," Jesse said.

"Did you ever actually work on a movie?"

"I worked homicide."

"So you were spared?"

"I was."

"And now you're a chief."

"Yes."

"With a great many important things to do."

"Not really. Mostly I write parking tickets."

"I find that hard to believe."

She took a sip of her wine.

"How does someone become a line producer," Jesse said.

"You're kidding, right?"

"No."

"You seriously want to know?"

"I do."

She looked at him skeptically.

"Okay," she said. "Just remember, you asked. I studied to be an accountant, like my dad. After graduation, he helped me get a job at Warner Brothers. My job was to track the daily information flow as it came in from the various movie sets, synthesize it, and then report it to the head of finance. My boss took a liking to me, and before long he upped me to the job of production accountant. I had to be on the set in order to keep careful track of how the money was being spent and then report it to the studio. Is this in the least bit interesting?"

"It is to me."

"Okay. Sorry. Accountants are generally considered to be notoriously dull."

Jesse smiled.

"It was important that I be privy to how every penny was being spent and why, because accuracy in reporting that information to the studio was critical. Over time, I worked closely with several of the studio's best line producers, and as a result, learned their job. I was in New Zealand with a small feature when midway through the shoot, the line producer suffered a heart attack. My boss back in Hollywood suggested that I step into the job. After all, I was on the scene and was an integral part of the process. I knew where all the bodies were buried, so to speak. It made sense. Plus, it was a chance to elevate myself. So I held my nose and jumped."

"How did it go?"

"I threw up several times each day, but I managed to finish the picture. I've been line producing ever since."

"I like a story with a happy ending."

"Let's wait until this one's in the can before we talk about happy endings. I still have Marisol Hinton in front of me."

"Meaning?"

"I worked with her once before."

"And you didn't like her?"

"It wasn't a question of liking her. Marisol is permanently tuned to the Marisol channel. All Marisol, all the time. Twenty-four-seven. No one else exists. Nothing else matters."

"So why are you working with her again?"

"She requested me."

"So she must have liked you."

"She and her husband both liked me. She didn't perceive me as a threat, so I passed muster."

"Her husband?"

"A small-time actor named Ryan Rooney. You ever hear of him?"

"Can't say that I have."

"Ryan Rooney was in *Tomorrow We Love* with her. They had the kind of torrid affair that she usually reserved only for members of the crew. Why, I don't know. He's as self-involved as she is. It beats me why they got married in the first place. She's highly competitive. I can't imagine her being helpful to him. Or to anyone, for that matter. It's been all downhill for him ever since."

"Is he in this movie?"

"God, no. Rumor is she accepted the part so she could get away from him. I read somewhere he had taken to smacking her around."

"Hooray for Hollywood," Jesse said.

After dinner, they walked the boardwalk to Frankie's rented waterfront apartment. The warmth of the day had given way to the chill of an early fall evening. She wrapped her coat more tightly around her. She clutched Jesse's arm as they walked.

The crisp smell of the sea rode in on the coattails of a steady, bracing wind. A galaxy of starlight lit up the cloudless sky. A lone figure walked hurriedly by them, his head lowered against the wind.

"Paradise is a long way from Hollywood," Frankie said.

"It's home for me now. I like where I live and how I live."

"Do you miss it?"

"L.A.?"

"Yes."

"Maybe the anonymity. It's hard for me to be private here."

"And that bothers you?"

"Sometimes."

"Because?"

"By nature I'm a hermit. I think I'd be happiest living in a cave and spending the winters in hibernation."

"It's hard for a police chief to be a hermit."

"Exactly," he said.

They had arrived at her building, a new five-story brick-and-glass modern overlooking the harbor. When they reached the main entrance, she turned to him.

"I had a lovely time, Jesse," she said.

"Me, too."

"Do you think we can do this again?"

"I do."

"Goody," she said.

10

Harry Kaplan, the process server, found Ryan Rooney in front of the trendy industry restaurant Craft, talking with a prospective agent, a toothy shark of a woman in her twenties, dressed entirely in black.

Kaplan interrupted them.

"Mr. Rooney," he said.

"Yes."

Kaplan pressed the summons into Rooney's hand.

"You've been served," he said, before disappearing into the crowd on the sidewalk.

Ryan shrugged.

"It was nice to meet you, Ryan," the woman said, and hurried away. Ryan watched her leave.

Then he opened the document and began to read. Several lines caught his eye.

"Marisol Hinton vs. Ryan Rooney..."

"Reference is made to the prenuptial agreement between the parties...."

"The aforementioned will immediately vacate the premises of the residence located at..."

"Mr. Rooney's executive position at Marisol Hinton Enterprises shall be deemed to have been terminated...."

"No further financial obligations regarding Mr. Rooney shall accrue either to Marisol Hinton or to Marisol Hinton Enterprises...."

Ryan folded the summons, put it in his pocket, walked to the parking lot, and got into his Prius. He sat there for a while, considering his options.

The prenup he had signed deprived him of access to any of Marisol's assets.

He had very little money, having mostly relied on her largesse for his expenses. He owned the Prius, but his insurance was due for renewal. Without work, his future was uncertain.

He was considering a move to New York, where he might find work in the theater and where Marisol's influence was less pervasive than it was in L.A. But he would require more cash to establish himself there.

He hoped she would stake him. One final gesture for old times' sake. He figured she owed him. After all, it was because of her that his career had stalled in the first place.

He switched on the Prius and pulled out of the parking lot onto Century Park Boulevard. The towering skyscrapers of Century City had long since replaced the back lot of Twentieth Century–Fox, which had originally stood there.

All that remained of William Fox's dream factory was a replica of a New York City street and an elevated train platform on which Barbra Streisand's *Hello, Dolly!* had been filmed.

He headed for the freeway, which would take him back to Camarillo, an industrial city located in the outer reaches of Los Angeles where he was staying in a low-rent residential motel managed by one of his would-be actor friends.

He thought about Marisol and his need for resettlement money. Surely she wouldn't refuse him. They were still married. The divorce papers had yet to be signed.

And if she said no? He'd deal with that if the time came. But he was already formulating a backup plan. One that would carry with it an exceptionally hefty price tag.

11

Jesse was sitting at his desk, sipping coffee, when Molly hollered, "Renzo Lazzeri on three."

Renzo Lazzeri owned the largest nursery in Paradise, which was once a factory warehouse that he had purchased when the factory closed its doors. He converted the space into a massive greenhouse, a showcase for every kind of garden and plant life indigenous to the Northeast. He added a landscape design department, which became notable for creating the most beautiful gardens in Paradise.

Grasses, saplings, hedges, bushes, seedlings, and flowers fought for space in his greenhouse. He specialized in rhododendrons and hydrangeas and also beach roses, which bloomed in profusion at all the best waterfront homes. And if you needed a riding mower or a top-of-the-line Weber grill, Renzo was your guy.

Jesse picked up the call.

"Renzo," he said.

"Jesse," Renzo said. "How the hell are you?"

"Better since I gave up hope."

Renzo's laughter filled Jesse's ear.

"To what do I owe the honor," Jesse said.

"Frankly, I didn't know who else to call."

"What's up?"

"This may sound strange, but I think I'm being cheated by Paradise Water and Power."

Jesse sat upright in his chair.

"How so," he said.

"I use a lot of water around here. Everything I have is always thirsty, so I keep an eye on my consumption levels. My manager regularly checks the meter readings. Lately he's noticed that our bills are larger than they were in the past. Not by a whole lot but noticeable."

"So what did you do?"

"I checked our meter readings against the meter readings on the invoices."

"And?"

"They were different."

"The meter readings on the invoices were different from the meter readings that your manager took?"

"They were higher."

"Indicating a greater water usage than what your readings reflected?"

"Yes."

"Did you do anything about it?"

"I asked my manager to call W and P and explain what he had discovered."

"And?"

"They told him that his readings were wrong."

"So what did you do?"

"I called you, of course."

"It's good to be the king," Jesse said.

"What should I do?"

"Leave it with me. Let me look into it."

"With pleasure."

"Yours isn't the first call I've had about this."

"So I'm not completely crazy?"

"I never said that."

12

On his way home, Jesse stopped at Assistant DA Marty Reagan's office.

Reagan was at his desk, in his shirtsleeves, poring over reams of material. File folders and legal briefs covered the desktop. Many were stacked in piles, several of which were overloaded and threatened to topple over.

Reagan removed his reading glasses and looked up at Jesse.

"We got slammed," he said. "Judge released her to her parents."

"What about the charges," Jesse said.

He picked up a stack of papers from the visitor's chair in front of Reagan's desk, placed them on the floor, and sat down.

"The driver of the Audi is awake," Reagan said. "He's got an awful headache, but he's alert and expected to make a complete recovery. He's refusing to press charges. When the DA heard that, he insisted we drop everything, too."

"Including the reckless endangerment?"

"Yes."

"Running a stop sign?"

"Yes."

"Resisting arrest?"

"Yes."

"The father, right?"

"I never said this, but it turns out he's a major contributor."

"To the DA?"

"He runs for the office every four years," Reagan said.

"So daddy's little angel gets to skate?"

"With a hundred-dollar fine for texting."

"Suspended license?"

"Judge waived that, too. You didn't hear it from me, but you can likely bet the farm that Mr. Cassidy assured the driver of the Audi that he would be generously taken care of."

Jesse sighed.

He reached over and picked up the stack of papers. He placed them back on the chair, stood up, and headed for the door.

"I'm sorry, Jesse," Reagan said.

"Thanks anyway, Marty."

Jesse reached for the doorknob.

"A word of advice?"

Jesse looked back at him.

"The DA thinks you should walk away from this."

"Excuse me?"

"I know you, Jesse. This isn't going to sit well with you. As your friend, I'm suggesting that you let it go. Don't be looking for any more trouble with the Cassidys. With the girl. Best to just drop it."

Jesse didn't say anything.

"Please don't do anything stupid, Jesse."

Jesse flashed him a lopsided grin.

"I mean it," Reagan said.

It was dark when Jesse got home. He turned on the lights and headed for the kitchen. He was intercepted by Mildred Memory, his cat, who circled him, rubbing herself against his legs, her tail upright and shimmying.

Mildred had become primarily an indoor cat, and a rather chubby one at that. Jesse constantly spoiled her. She responded by behaving like an imperious hausfrau.

Jesse opened a can of her favorite food and scooped half of it into her bowl. Then he filled a glass with ice and poured himself a scotch.

He sat down heavily on one of his two armchairs, took a healthy sip of the scotch, and considered the events of the day.

The Courtney Cassidy experience was unsettling. Authority in the service of unbridled riches never failed to raise his hackles. Marty Reagan was right when he predicted it wouldn't sit well with him. It didn't.

He thought about Frankie Greenberg. She was smart and attractive. She was interesting, and he was interested. His recent adventure with Alexis Richardson had ended when she left town. He and Sunny Randall remained apart. He'd been alone for a while, and he was restless.

He yawned.

He drained his glass, then turned off the lights and went upstairs, Mildred following closely behind.

By the time he had changed and got into bed, she'd pretty much taken it over. He picked her up, lay down, and planted her beside him. She stood up and glared at him. Then she climbed onto his chest, circled twice, lay down, and fell asleep.

He was able to reach over and turn off the light, but he was now forced to sleep on his back, with Mildred's burgeoning girth freighting him down.

"Aw, hell," he said, squirming. But after a while he, too, fell asleep.

13

esse was parked across the street from the Cassidy estate, which was located on the South Shore, spread across twenty acres of prime beachfront property.

The Cassidys had razed the estate's original house, a sprawling shingled Colonial, and in its place had erected an oversized postmodern featuring a pair of extended wings off the main house, each containing lavishly appointed guest suites and an exercise room.

They had also added an Olympic-size swimming pool, two tennis courts, a putting green, and servants' quarters.

Between the beach and the pool they had constructed a cabana that housed separate dressing-room facilities for men, women, and children. It contained a game room, a TV room, and a card room with a full-size bar.

The estate's big gates swung open, and a Lexus convertible turned onto Beach Road, heading toward town.

Courtney Cassidy was at the wheel, holding a cell phone to her ear. Which was illegal.

Jesse fired up his cruiser and followed her. She was driving above the speed limit, oblivious to the fact that she was being followed by a police cruiser. She continued to talk on her phone.

After a while, Jesse hit the siren and lights. He saw Courtney look in her rearview mirror. He beeped the siren a few times, signaling for her to pull over.

When both vehicles were stopped on the shoulder, Jesse got out of his cruiser and walked to the Lexus. Courtney lowered her window as he approached.

"License and registration," he said.

She stared at him.

"You again," she said. "What do you want this time?"

"Your license and registration, please. And while you're at it, hand me your phone, too."

"Why?"

"It's illegal in Massachusetts for anyone under the age of eighteen to talk on a handheld device while driving."

"Everyone knows that's a stupid law."

"It's a law, however, regardless of your personal lack of regard for it."

"I suppose you're gonna arrest me again."

"No. I'm going to cite you for breaking the law. And I'm going to confiscate your phone."

"Must you?"

Jesse didn't say anything.

She removed the license from her wallet and handed it to him.

"Registration," Jesse said.

"It's in here somewhere. Do I really have to find it?"

"You do if you don't want to spend the next several hours in jail."

She glared at him, then started searching for the registration slip.

"Cell phone," he said.

"What?"

"Give me your phone."

"No."

"Don't force me to arrest you again."

She sighed.

She gave him the phone.

"Everyone talks on their cell phones," she said.

"Didn't yesterday teach you anything?"

"Like what?"

"Like how driving while distracted can cause accidents and seriously injure people."

He stepped away from her car and began writing the citation.

She returned her license to her wallet and the registration slip to the glove box.

She muttered the word "shithead" under her breath.

He heard her.

"You talking to me," Jesse said.

"I didn't say anything."

He stepped closer to the car and stared at her. Then he handed her the citation.

"What do I do with this?"

"What it says to do."

"How about I just give it to my father."

"You can give it to the tooth fairy, for all I care."

He smiled at her.

"Have a nice day," he said.

14

Ryan followed Marisol's black Range Rover as it pulled through the gates into the driveway of her Beverly Hills mansion. He'd been parked down the street, waiting for her, sailing on a crystal meth high.

She had stopped taking his calls, and it had occurred to him that this might be his only opportunity to speak with her.

By the time Marisol saw him approaching, it was too late for her to reach the house or get back into her car.

He grabbed her arm.

"I'm sorry," he said. "You gave me no choice."

"Let go of me," she said, trying to wrest herself free.

"I want you to forgive me," he said, tightening his grip.

"You're frightening me, Ryan."

"That's not my intention."

"Let go of me."

"I'm not going to hurt you."

He let her go.

She stepped backward, massaging her arm.

"I know things haven't gone well with us," he said. "I did things I'm ashamed of. I beg your forgiveness."

"My forgiveness?"

"Yes."

"Come off it, Ryan."

"No, I mean it."

"What do you really want?"

"I want us to be friends."

"Friends? How could you even think such a thing?"

She glared at him. He reached over and caressed her face. She cringed.

"I need a favor," he said.

She didn't say anything.

"I want to leave California. I want to start fresh. In New York."

"What's stopping you?"

"I'm broke."

"That's not my problem."

"I know," he said, growing agitated. "But I'm asking you to help me."

"Help you how?"

"I need twenty-five thousand dollars. To get me to New York. To get me settled there. To allow me to live while I start over."

"You want me to give you twenty-five thousand dollars?"

"Yes."

She didn't say anything.

"We had some good times, Marisol. We even loved each other. What's done is done. Just this one favor. Please. I'll never bother you again."

She thought about it.

"All right," she said.

"You'll give me the money?"

"Yes."

"Now?"

"I don't keep that kind of cash around."

"You could write me a check."

"All right," she said, after a moment.

She reached into her purse, took out her checkbook, and wrote one for twenty-five thousand dollars. She handed it to him.

He looked at it. He put it in his pocket.

"Please leave now," she said.

He nodded.

He turned and walked to his car. "Thank you," he said, looking back to her. But by then she had made it safely into the house.

15

Jesse pulled to a stop in front of the Community Services Building, a Federal-style red-brick behemoth, built in the early 1900s as the original Paradise High School. It was now home to several municipal offices, including the Department of Water and Power.

Jesse entered the office of William J. Goodwin, the longtime DWP commissioner. Goodwin had held the position since the mid-1980s, making him the longest-serving public official in Paradise.

He and Jesse had met on a number of official occasions. Goodwin was a tiny man, quiet and unassuming. He dressed immaculately, favoring expensive suits worn with bow ties.

He spoke in a high-pitched tenor that often made him the butt of ill-intentioned humor.

Behind the desk in the outer office sat Ida Fearnley, Goodwin's longtime assistant.

Miss Fearnley was a large woman in middle age, well known for the shortness of her patience and the tartness of her tongue.

"Chief Stone," she said to Jesse. "What a nice surprise."

"Miss Fearnley," he said. "Still guarding the fort, I see."

"In a manner of speaking."

"And life remains good up here at W and P?"

"It's pretty much the same as always. How can we help you?"

"I'm sorry to show up unannounced, but I wonder if the commissioner might have a few minutes to spare."

"He's in there. Let me go see what he's up to."

She left him and entered the commissioner's office.

Jesse walked the outer office, glancing at the many citations and awards on the office walls. Most reflected appreciation for Mr. Goodwin's long years of service.

The door to his office opened, and William J. Goodwin appeared.

"Chief Stone," he said. "An unexpected pleasure. Do come in. Can we get you anything?"

"Thank you, no," Jesse said.

The two men shook hands, and Goodwin gestured for Jesse to enter ahead of him.

Goodwin's office looked like the set of a London men's club in a forties movie. Lots of leather and mahogany.

He ushered Jesse to a pair of glossy brown leather armchairs. They sat. Goodwin's feet barely touched the floor.

"I'm sorry to be a bother, Mr. Goodwin," Jesse said, "but I've recently had some inquiries regarding your department, and I thought it better to direct them to the source."

"Me being the source?"

"Exactly."

"To what inquiries are you referring?"

"Do you know of any recent rate increases regarding water usage?"

"None. We purchase our water directly from the Commonwealth of Massachusetts, and the rates have been constant for quite some time. I can't say I agree with the state's decision to maintain these rate levels, but clearly my opinions count for very little."

"What are your opinions," Jesse said.

"It's my belief that our society has little respect for this most precious of our natural resources. We use it capriciously and wastefully. When you consider the shortage of potable water on our planet and the manner in which we squander our share of it, I find it shameful that it costs so little, the result of which allows us to deplete our supplies as recklessly as we wish."

Jesse didn't say anything.

"My beliefs, however, go largely ignored at state," Goodwin said. "Try as I may to voice them."

"What would you have them do?"

"I'd have them charge a usage rate that would force restraint.

One out of every seven people on the planet doesn't have access to clean water. Unless things change, we'll soon be facing a global disaster."

"Sounds like a problem for the environmentalists."

"The environmentalists have become so politicized that it's impossible for them to argue such an issue without the concurrence of lobbyists and power brokers. Electability is all that these morons care about."

"This is all above my pay grade," Jesse said. "For what it's worth, I agree with you. I'm afraid, however, that I'm only here to determine whether or not any rate hikes have occurred in Paradise."

"Would that that were the case. But, alas, it's not."

Jesse stood.

"Thank you for your time, Mr. Goodwin. And for sharing your insights."

"My irrelevant insights," Goodwin said.

16

Ryan drove directly from the mansion to Marisol's bank. He handed the check to the teller and asked her to cash it. She examined it and said, "I can't authorize this much cash on my own. I need to speak to my manager."

He nodded.

She locked the cash drawer and left her station.

Ryan stood waiting at the window for an inordinately long time.

Then the teller returned, accompanied by a severe-looking older man. The man stepped to the window.

"You're Ryan Rooney," he said.

"Yes."

"A stop-payment order has been placed on this check."

"What do you mean?"

"I mean that the check is no good."

"What do you mean it's no good. I just received it."

"Be that as it may, I'm unable to cash it."

Ryan raised his voice. "It is good," he said. "I just got it. Give me my money."

Ryan was attracting the attention of other bank customers.

"Please lower your voice," the man said.

"I want my money," Ryan said loudly.

The man looked at him. Then he signaled to the bank guard, who was already headed in their direction.

"I'm afraid I'll have to ask you to leave," the man said.

"Not until you give me my money," Ryan said.

"Harold," the manager said to the guard, "would you please escort Mr. Rooney from the premises."

Ryan was enraged.

"I'm not leaving until I get my money," he said.

The guard grabbed Ryan's arm and twisted it up behind his back, which caused Ryan to cry out in pain. He clamped his other hand on Ryan's neck and hustled him out of the building. Once outside, he shoved Ryan away.

As he struggled to gain traction, Ryan lost his footing and stumbled. He fell to the pavement, ripping his pants leg as he landed. He leapt back up and made a move toward the guard.

Then he heard the sound of sirens in the distance. He stopped and listened as they drew closer.

He wheeled around and walked quickly to his Prius. He jumped in and swung it out of the parking lot, moments before a police cruiser pulled in.

This isn't over, he thought.

17

Molly wandered into Jesse's office. He was seated behind his desk, staring out the window. He turned around when he heard her come in.

"There's good news and bad news," she said.

"Okay," Jesse said.

"Do you want to know which is which?"

"Have I a choice?"

"The bad news is Carter Hansen wants to see you."

"And the good news?"

"I'm having an excellent hair day."

I've already had two calls from Portia Cassidy," Carter Hansen said. "She appears to be out for blood."

"How so," Jesse said.

"She thinks you're terrorizing her daughter."

They were sitting in Hansen's office. He had reluctantly provided Jesse with some coffee.

"Courtney Cassidy is an unrepentant, obnoxious adolescent who seems to take a perverse pleasure in breaking the law."

"What were you doing in front of her house this morning?"

"Sightseeing," Jesse said.

"I wish I found your attempts at humor amusing. Were you stalking the girl?"

"I was surveilling."

"Stop being obtuse. What were you doing in front of her house?"

"I suspected that Ms. Cassidy was a chronic abuser of the law, and I was right. She was talking on a cell phone when she drove past me."

"So what? People drive and talk on cell phones all the time."

"It's against the law."

"Everyone knows it's a dumb law."

"But it's state law nonetheless. You could look it up."

"So you ticketed her?"

"I did. Her driver's license can now be revoked for a period of six months. She's a two-time offender."

"And you believe that a judge will actually revoke her license?"

"An honest one will."

"Oh, please," Hansen said. "I want you to stop harassing her. It's bad for business."

" 'Harassing her'?"

"Yes."

"Are you instructing me to look the other way when a crime is being committed?"

Hansen didn't say anything.

"This girl has already been the cause of an accident that seriously injured someone, to which she responded in an arrogant and willful manner. I will continue to challenge her until the authorities can no longer afford to ignore her."

"Don't," Hansen said.

"Excuse me?"

"Don't keep challenging her."

Jesse stood.

"We're done here," Jesse said. "As we have previously discussed, your position enables you to fire me but not to tell me what to do."

Hansen looked away.

"Unless you're firing me, I'm going back to work."

Hansen didn't say anything.

"Stay out of it, Carter," Jesse said. "You don't need any part of this fur ball."

Hansen watched as Jesse left his office.

18

Jesse pulled into the driveway of the Wilburforce School, where Courtney Cassidy was a student.

After waiting in his outer office for several minutes, Jesse was ushered into the office of the principal, Dr. Rodger Pike.

Pike was a portly, fiftyish man, a pipe smoker who was still fretting over the school policy that prevented him from lighting up indoors. To compensate, he picked up his pipe and placed it in the corner of his mouth.

"What can I do for you, Chief Stone," he said, sucking on the pipe.

"I'm sorry to disturb you on such short notice, Dr. Pike, but I have a couple of questions regarding one of your students."

"Of course," Pike said. "Which student?"

"Courtney Cassidy."

"Just so you understand, Chief Stone, our student information is confidential."

"I've recently had a couple of run-ins with Ms. Cassidy, and I'm curious about her."

" 'Run-ins'?"

"Yesterday she was the cause of a rather serious traffic accident. She was driving and texting. Today I cited her for driving while talking on a cell phone. I'm concerned that she might be a danger to herself, as well as to the community."

"What is it you want from me," Dr. Pike said.

"Answers to some questions."

"I'll try."

"What kind of student is she?"

"Meaning?"

"Meaning are her grades good? Is she well behaved? Does she obey the rules? Is she in any way difficult?"

Dr. Pike removed the pipe from his mouth and returned it to his desk. He carefully wiped his mouth with a handkerchief. He stood up, walked to his office door, and softly closed it. He then returned to the desk.

"Your reputation precedes you, Chief Stone. My understanding is that you have a noble track record when it comes to dealing with delinquent juveniles. For that reason, and not for attribution, I will tell you that the Wilburforce School has had its share of difficulties with Courtney Cassidy. She is resistant to authority. She has issues with her peers. She is frequently sullen and uncooperative."

"Why do you keep her?"

"Her father is the school's largest contributor."

"Aaah," Jesse said.

"Aaah, indeed," Dr. Pike said.

"Thank you for your frankness."

"It's really a shame."

"What is?"

"Off the record, she's generally a pain in the ass. But I somehow believe she's not a bad girl at heart. Were I a psychiatrist, I might even suggest that she's acting out a desperate need for attention."

"Is she a good student?"

"Heavens, no."

"Does she socialize?"

"Meaning?"

"Does she have many friends? Any boyfriends?"

"Again, I'm not really at liberty to say. Off the record, however, she does get along with a number of the other girls, but not the truly popular ones. No boyfriends that I know of."

"Thank you again for your candor," Jesse said, standing.

"I do hope you can help this child," Dr. Pike said.

"I do hope this child can be helped," Jesse said.

19

Molly handed Jesse his phone messages as he walked by her desk.

"Frankie Greenberg called," she said.

He nodded and went into his office.

He returned her call first.

"Help," she said.

"'Help'?"

"Marisol Hinton arrives tomorrow. I need a respite."

"'A respite'?"

"Stop repeating everything I say. I need relief. I need to feel the wind in my hair. I need to be lifted off the earth and transported to a magical land where nymphs play and angels sing."

"I know just the place."

"You do?"

"Yes."

"Where?"

"My house," he said.

"What time?"

This is just what I'd imagined," Frankie said as she entered the house. Jesse ushered her into the living room, where she dropped her things on a chair.

She looked around. The kitchen caught her attention.

"You're cooking?"

"No."

"You're kidding, right," she said, inhaling deeply.

"Vito Rezza did the cooking," Jesse said.

"Who's Vito Rezza?"

"The owner of Vito's Ristorante, of course."

Frankie looked at him questioningly. "On tonight's menu, we have a Caprese salad, along with freshly baked garlic bread. Our entrée is veal piccata served on a bed of linguini *aglio e olio*. And for dessert we have Vito's legendary tiramisu."

"Wow," she said. Jesse grabbed a pair of wineglasses and poured an already decanted Lungarotti Rubesco.

"This is fabulous," she said, after tasting it.

"Respite enough?"

"Pinch me, I'm dreaming."

Jesse took her wineglass and put it down on the counter. Then he put his arms around her and kissed her.

"Wow again," she said.

"And we haven't even gotten to the appetizers."

He kissed her again, then paused.

"We have a dilemma," Jesse said, leaning back slightly.

"Oh?"

"Although we have an amazing dinner simmering on the stove, in point of fact, it could benefit from simmering a bit longer."

"How much longer?"

"If I showed you around upstairs, it's entirely possible we might become distracted long enough to allow it to simmer to maturity."

"By all means."

"By all means what?"

"Take me upstairs."

"With pleasure," he said.

Frankie was swimming in Jesse's extra-large white cotton bathrobe, which she wore with the sleeves rolled up past her elbows. Jesse had on a gray PPD sweatshirt and a pair of blue-and-green-checked pajama bottoms.

Having finished the salad, they now eagerly worked on the

veal and the pasta. Frankie was sipping the Rubesco. Jesse had switched to Sam Adams Winter Lager.

Saving the tiramisu for later, they retired to the living room, where Jesse settled himself into one of his armchairs. Frankie made herself comfortable on his lap.

Mildred Memory was camped out on the adjacent chair, watching them through half-closed eyes.

Frankie put her arms around Jesse's neck and rested her head on his shoulder.

"I think I've just discovered the meaning of life," she said.

Jesse kissed the top of her head. She looked up at him and raised her face to his.

"I could get used to this," she said.

She kissed him once, then again with urgency.

She adjusted herself on the chair until she was straddling him. They stayed that way for some time.

20

Jesse saw Courtney's Lexus pull into the Wilburforce School parking lot from his spot across the street. She negotiated the left turn while holding her cell phone to her ear.

Jesse stepped out of his cruiser and walked to the lot. Courtney was slowly circling it, looking for a parking space. When she spotted him, she slammed on her brakes and dropped the phone.

Jesse approached the car, and when he was beside it, he motioned for her to get out. She opened the door and stepped out.

"What," she said.

"Pick up the phone and hand it to me."

"Pick it up yourself."

Jesse noticed that they had attracted the attention of a number of students, who milled around, watching.

"Please hand me your driver's license and your car keys."

"Why?"

"Because you have now officially lost your right to operate a motor vehicle."

"What are you talking about?"

"License and keys," Jesse said.

"No," she said.

Jesse took out his cell phone and punched in a number. When Molly answered, he asked her which officer was closest to the Wilburforce School. When she named Rich Bauer, Jesse instructed her to have him get to the school parking lot as quickly as possible.

Then he stood silently, staring at Courtney.

She became uneasy. She was the centerpiece of a spectacle that was now appearing before nearly half the student body.

"What's going on," she said.

Jesse didn't respond.

Within moments, Bauer's cruiser entered the lot, siren blaring. He pulled to within inches of where Jesse was standing and got out of the car.

"What's up, Skipper?"

"Please take Ms. Cassidy into custody, read her her rights and then escort her to jail."

"You can't do that," Courtney said. "I'm at school."

"Do it, Rich," Jesse said.

Bauer approached Courtney, who backed away. He was forced to follow her until she finally stood still. Then he took his handcuffs from his service belt and cuffed her.

She started to cry.

After he read Courtney her rights, he walked her to his cruiser and placed her in the backseat. Then he got in and drove away.

Jesse phoned the station.

When Molly answered, he said, "Have Smitty come and impound Courtney's Lexus, which is in the parking lot of the Wilburforce School."

"Oh, baby," Molly said.

Jesse didn't say anything.

"I'm on it," she said.

Jesse looked around at the gawkers.

"Break it up," he shouted. "It's over."

The students began to disperse.

Jesse retrieved an evidence bag from his cruiser. He put on a rubber glove and picked up Courtney's cell phone. He placed it in the evidence bag.

He called the DA's office.

Smitty's flatbed was just pulling into the parking lot as Jesse was leaving. He handed the car keys to the driver. Then he walked back across the street, got into his cruiser, and drove away.

Third offense," Jesse said to DA Aaron Silver.

They were sitting in Silver's office, accompanied by Marty Reagan.

"I thought Marty asked you to drop this," Silver said.

"I'll ignore that remark," Jesse said.

Silver sighed.

"I'll settle for a one-year suspension of her driving privileges, which is state law," Jesse said. "Also, the largest fine allowable."

Silver didn't say anything.

"Probation would also be good. It would keep her in the system and place her under our supervision."

"Meaning," Reagan said.

"Community service might prove invaluable to this child. Give her the opportunity to see how things really are."

"No judge would sanction it," Silver said.

"I'd like a hearing just the same," Jesse said. "Perhaps I could convince him. Or her."

"I'll see what I can do," Silver said.

Jesse sat for a while.

"What," Reagan said.

"It's as if she can't control herself," Jesse said. "She appears to be demanding attention and doing it in a way that can't be ignored."

"I said I'd see what I can do," Aaron Silver said.

"Just do the right thing," Jesse said. "We've got a troubled kid on our hands."

21

Richard and Portia Cassidy were waiting for Jesse at the station. They exuded money and breeding and a kind of arrogance that Jesse found offensive. He asked them to join him in his office.

Richard wore his black pin-striped Brooks Brothers suit well, but Jesse wondered why not even a single strand of his abundant salt-and-pepper hair was out of place. Had to be some kind of spray, he figured.

Portia was a handsome woman who might once have been beautiful. But Jesse saw that her looks had been augmented by plastic surgery. Her lips were drawn tight, and her skin appeared as if it had been ironed.

"May I offer you anything," Jesse said as he stepped behind his desk.

"I'd like some coffee," Mr. Cassidy said.

"Mrs. Cassidy?"

"I'd like your head on a platter," she said.

Jesse looked at her.

Then he called for Molly, who appeared in the office doorway.

"Will you bring Mr. Cassidy a coffee, please," he said.

"How do you take it," she said.

"Black would be fine." Molly left.

"We're out of platters," Jesse said to Portia.

"Don't be impudent with me, Chief Stone," she said.

"Jesse," he said.

"Excuse me?"

"My name is Jesse."

"Can you believe this guy," Portia said to her husband.

"What brings you here," Jesse said.

"You know damned well what brings us here," Portia said.

Molly entered with the coffee and handed it to Richard.

"Thank you," Richard said to her.

To Jesse he said, "I understand you've arrested Courtney again. Isn't this all a bit much?"

"Your daughter seems to delight in breaking the law and then flaunting it. Within a matter of days she's become a three-time offender and appears to be either oblivious of that fact or proud of it."

"You're harassing her," Portia said. "You're purposely singling her out."

Jesse looked at her.

"You do know that she narrowly escaped with her life in a traffic accident that she caused," he said.

"Says you," Portia said.

"Please, Portia," Richard said. "This won't get us anywhere. What is it you want, Chief Stone?"

"Your daughter needs some serious discipline."

"We'll be the judge of that," Richard said.

"You've already lost that privilege," Jesse said. "She'll be judged by the court now."

"She's seventeen years old," Richard said. "She's a minor. Nothing will come of this, I can assure you."

"The law is clear about the penalties attached to cell-phone usage while driving."

"And?"

"At the very least, your daughter's right to drive is going to be suspended."

"That's a crock," Portia said.

"And because she's a three-time offender, this office is going to petition the court to have her placed on probation."

"I've heard enough from this bastard," Portia said as she stood. "I'm going after your head, Chief Stone. And you haven't experienced the wrath of anyone like me before."

"Have you always had head issues, Mrs. Cassidy?"

"Excuse me?"

"That's the second time you singled out my head. I was just wondering if perhaps you had some kind of fixation."

"There's no talking to this asshole," she said to her husband.

Richard Cassidy sighed.

"I suppose this isn't over," he said.

"You bet your sweet bippy it's not," Jesse said.

22

Jesse pulled his cruiser to a stop behind the orange-and-blue Water and Power truck that was parked on South Halsey Street.

He got out of his car and leaned heavily against the front fender, facing the sun, hoping to acquire even the slightest suggestion of a tan.

Oscar LaBrea appeared from the back of the house. When he spotted the cruiser, he headed to where Jesse was sunning himself.

"You looking for me," he said.

Jesse continued to aim his face at the sun.

"Here I live in a seaside community and have no color whatsoever," he said. "I'm trying to rectify that."

Neither of them said anything.

After a while, LaBrea said, "Was it me you were looking for?"

"You Oscar LaBrea?"

LaBrea was a big pasty-faced man in his mid-forties. He wore yellow overalls emblazoned with the DWP logo. He had on an expensive pair of Oakley sunglasses.

"Am I in some kind of trouble," he said.

"Not at all. I'm Jesse Stone, by the way."

He extended his hand.

"I know who you are," LaBrea said, taking it. "Is there something you wanted?"

"Mind if I ask you a few questions?"

Oscar shrugged.

"You read water meters for the DWP," Jesse said.

"For the past twelve years."

"Good job?"

"I like it."

"Tough job?"

"Sometimes."

"How so?"

"Restricted access. Dogs. Dissatisfied customers. That sort of thing."

" 'Dissatisfied customers'?"

"On occasion," LaBrea said.

"What makes for a dissatisfied customer?"

"I don't know. People who think they're paying too much. Who disagree with their bill."

"Why would someone disagree with a DWP bill?"

"Any number of reasons."

"Such as?"

"They don't believe they used as much water as they were billed for. They think they've been overcharged."

"Are they ever right about that?"

"Not often."

"Do people who disagree with a meter reading ever contact the department and challenge those readings?"

"Sometimes."

"What happens in a case like that?"

"They're wrong is what happens."

"Is it possible they could be right?"

"Not likely."

"But possible?"

"What is it you're saying?"

"That a meter might register higher amounts of water usage than what the customer actually purchased."

"Are you suggesting meter tampering?"

"I'm not suggesting anything," Jesse said. "I'm fact-finding, is all."

Oscar LaBrea stood silently for a while. Then he started walking toward his vehicle.

"Where are you going?"

"I think I don't want to talk to you anymore," LaBrea said.

"Why not?"

"I want to talk with my lawyer."

"Your lawyer?"

"Yes."

"Why on earth would you want to talk with your lawyer?"

LaBrea didn't say anything. He opened the door to his truck and climbed in. He looked back at Jesse, then started the engine and pulled away.

Jesse watched him leave.

23

The cocktail party honoring Marisol Hinton was just gathering steam when Jesse stopped by.

A collection of actors, assorted movie brass, and several members of the staff and crew had been invited to the small gathering that Carter Hansen was hosting at Noah's Ark, a colorful theme park of a saloon located on the Paradise waterfront.

The locals referred to it as the "twofer bar." Noah's offered two drinks for the price of one; two appetizers, both soup and salad; two sides with each entrée; and a pair of desserts as well.

The staff and crew had converged at the bar, taking advantage of Hansen's largesse. Noah's mojitos were very much in demand, but the prop mistress had seductively convinced the bartender to concoct several pitchers of Long Island iced tea, which were disappearing fast.

The actors had taken over the buffet, treating themselves to hors d'oeuvres and wine. Noah's shrimp boats, served two at a time, were a big favorite.

Selectmen Hansen, Comden, and Hasty Hathaway were among the celebrants. A handful of local merchants and other town luminaries were also there.

Jesse saw Frankie Greenberg standing at one of the tables, beside Marisol, who was nervously scanning the room with eyes that reflected both tension and discomfort. She seemed taken aback by being the focus of so many of those in the room, yet at the same time she appeared needful of that focus.

Marisol's was a classic cinematic face. She had a prominent forehead, widely spaced large blue eyes, and sharply pronounced cheekbones. Hers was a ski nose, curling cutely upward at its tip. She had oversized lips and a notable jaw. Taken independently, her features seemed oddly incongruous. But seen through the lens of a camera, they coalesced perfectly, transforming her into movie-star beautiful.

Frankie waved to Jesse, who picked his way through the crowd toward her.

"This is who I was telling you about," Frankie said to Marisol. "Jesse Stone, meet Marisol Hinton."

Marisol turned her blue-eyed gaze to Jesse.

"So you're the famous police chief," she said.

"Serving and protecting."

"Frankie said you used to be a cop in Los Angeles."

"I was a homicide detective."

"Homicide? You mean murder?"

"Yes."

"A lot of that going around in Los Angeles."

"There is."

"Frankie said . . . I mean, I wonder . . ."

Her voice trailed off.

After an awkward pause, Jesse said, "What do you wonder?"

Marisol shifted uneasily.

"May I speak candidly, Chief Stone?"

"Jesse," he said.

"Jesse," she said. "May I?"

"Of course."

"It's about my husband."

Jesse didn't say anything.

"My husband and I are estranged. He had become violent, and I couldn't handle it any longer. So I changed the locks and threw him out. He still frightens me, though. I thought I'd be all right once I got here, but now I find that I'm not."

"He isn't here in Paradise, is he?"

"No. But I'm terrified that he might show up."

She looked at Jesse imploringly. Either she was actually frightened or she was an exceptionally good actress. Jesse wasn't certain which.

"He calls me a lot. At all hours. He keeps telling me how angry he is. He's always yelling. I just don't know what to do."

"Why not change your number?"

"He'd still find me."

"How about I provide you with a secure phone," Jesse said.

Marisol looked at him.

"'A secure phone'?"

"A special police phone."

"And you'd give me one?"

"I'd lend you one."

"A police phone?"

"Yes."

"For how long?"

"For as long as you're here."

"And the number would be private?"

"Yes."

"And he couldn't trace it."

"Correct."

"You'd actually do that?"

"I would."

"That would be amazingly helpful," she said, a smile appearing on her face. "I'd really appreciate that. I would be in your debt."

"That wouldn't be necessary. Hopefully it'll help ease your fears," he said.

Jesse looked over at Frankie, who eyed him apologetically.

"I'll see to it," he said.

He excused himself, shook Marisol's hand, and as he left, he gave Frankie's arm a barely noticeable squeeze.

She smiled.

Once outside, Jesse took a deep breath. He was about to jump into his cruiser when Suitcase joined him.

"So what's she like," Suitcase said.

"She's frightened."

"Frightened?"

"Of her husband."

"Ryan Rooney?"

"Yes."

"Because?"

"She says he's become violent."

"Yikes."

"Exactly. I need you to do something, Suit."

"What?"

"I need you to give her one of our encrypted cell phones."

"Marisol Hinton?"

"Yes."

"One of our secure phones?"

"Yes."

"Aren't they for departmental use only?"

"Yes."

"And you want me to give one to Marisol Hinton?"

"A loaner."

Suitcase didn't say anything.

Jesse didn't say anything.

"You could get in trouble for this," Suitcase said.

"I'll take my chances," Jesse said.

———

Jesse was sitting in the living room, scotch in hand, when his cell phone rang.

"What did you think," Frankie said.

"She's very frightened."

"She has me worried."

"I can understand why."

"I've never seen her like this before."

"You might want to consider providing her with some personal security."

"We already have one of our officers assigned to her."

"I'm not talking about movie cops. I mean genuine security. More exclusive and more arduously trained than the average cop who services a movie set."

"Are you suggesting a bodyguard?"

"I'm suggesting a tactical security officer."

"What's that?"

"Someone highly skilled in the serious business of providing personal protection. A person with martial arts expertise, knowledgeable about weaponry and trained in the finer points of security."

"You know someone like that?"

"I might."

"Would he be expensive?"

"Yes."

"Would the movie be responsible for paying him?"

"I wouldn't know about that. But when I was in L.A., I knew a handful of qualified operatives whose job it was to provide protection services to top-tier movie actors. There's always an obsessed clown or two out there who believes that it's his or her destiny to marry some media star and who will stop at nothing to get next to that star. Think Madonna. Jennifer Aniston. David Letterman. All of them victims of deranged stalkers. It's a whole lot more efficient to hire someone genuinely qualified to deal with these head cases than it is to leave it to some inexperienced rent-a-cop."

"I don't know if we can even afford it."

"Let me see if the guy I'm thinking about is even available," Jesse said. "Then you can worry about affording it. But I'll bet you have a few bucks stashed away in one of your general accounts that you can surreptitiously latch on to."

"You're smarter than you look."

"No one ever suffered from being underestimated," he said.

24

"ow may I help you," said the voice on the other end of the line.

"No 'How nice it is to hear from you,'" Jesse said.

"It's nice," the voice said. "What do you want?"

"You interested in a job?"

"It depends."

"On?"

"The job."

Jesse explained the job and the circumstances. And who it was that required his services.

"Why me?"

"Nobody better."

"You noticed."

"Be hard not to."

"Salary?"

"Negotiable." There was silence for a while.

"So," Jesse said.

"I'll be there tomorrow."

'll check to make sure he's in," Ida Fearnley said, somewhat less friendly than she was previously.

After several moments, she emerged from Commissioner Goodwin's office.

"He'll see you," she said.

Jesse went inside. William J. Goodwin was standing behind his desk, all four feet seven of him.

"Twice in one week," he said. "That's a record."

"Thank you for seeing me."

"What can I do for you now?"

"I'm afraid I'm here for the same reason I was last time."

"Water rates?"

"Yes. I had an unsettling conversation with one of your employees. Oscar LaBrea."

"Why would you be talking with Oscar LaBrea?"

"Follow-up," Jesse said.

"Follow-up to what?"

"To the conversation I had with you."

"You talked with one of our employees?"

"Yes."

"Why?"

"Because the issue of possible meter tampering hasn't gone away."

"Meter tampering, is it," Goodwin said.

Jesse didn't say anything.

"You suspect this department of engaging in meter tampering?"

"I don't suspect anyone of anything. I'm fact-finding, is all."

"And what facts did you learn from Mr. LaBrea?"

"Nothing specific, but I found his response to my visit unsettling."

"Oh?"

"He became evasive, and at one point, he broke off the conversation and told me he needed to speak with his lawyer."

"Why would he do that?"

"That was going to be one of my questions to you," Jesse said.

Goodwin didn't say anything.

"Why do you suppose Mr. LaBrea said that," Jesse said.

"I wouldn't know."

"Why would he need a lawyer?"

"I said I wouldn't know."

"Is he a trustworthy employee?"

"He's worked here for twelve years."

"How well do you know him?"

"Why would you ask me that?"

Jesse didn't respond.

"Do you suspect me of something," Goodwin said, drawing himself up to his full height.

"Why would you think that?"

"Because I don't like the tone of your questioning."

"Mr. Goodwin," Jesse said, "I've received complaints regarding possible irregularities at Paradise DWP. I'm here in response to those complaints. It's part of my job. I'm simply trying to determine what happened."

"And you think that somehow I'm involved in meter tampering?"

"I never said that."

"But you think that."

"I don't think anything except that both Mr. LaBrea and now you are behaving in a puzzling manner."

"This meeting is over, Chief Stone," Goodwin said. "If you have any further questions, please forward them to the DWP legal department. Hopefully you'll find satisfaction in their responses. Good day, sir."

Jesse stared at Goodwin for a while.

Goodwin shifted his feet uneasily.

"I said good day, Chief Stone."

Jesse left without responding.

25

Jesse parked his cruiser near the entrance to the footbridge that led to his house.

Wilson Cromartie was leaning against the railing, watching a flock of gulls as they made their way across the horizon, occasionally dipping into the sea in search of prey. He looked up when he heard Jesse approach.

"How," he said, raising his palm.

Jesse smiled.

Crow was a full-blooded Apache, well over six feet tall, dressed casually but elegantly. He wore a white shirt, pressed jeans, polished boots, and a silver concho belt. He was inordinately handsome, and he moved with an easy grace. He was all angles and planes, as if he had been packed very tightly into himself. His muscles bulged against his taut skin like sharp corners. Everything about him spoke of tightly compressed force.

"So when do I get to meet her?"

"Now, if you want."

"It's not every day that a humble Indian brave gets to rub elbows with a real-life movie star," he said.

"So long as that's all you rub," Jesse said.

Frankie was in her motor home, sorting through a huge stack of bills, when Jesse and Crow showed up.

"You're the bodyguard," she said to Crow.

"I'm Wilson Cromartie. On occasion I perform services as a personal security specialist."

Frankie looked at him.

"And you're interested in performing these services for Marisol Hinton."

"Not until I meet her."

"And if the meeting goes well?"

"Then perhaps I'll accept the assignment. Provided the money's right."

"What's right?"

Crow mentioned a number.

Frankie gulped.

"Have you any credentials which I might present to her," she said.

"No."

"No credentials?"

Crow didn't say anything.

"I see," she said.

She looked at Jesse, who shrugged.

"Would you like to meet her?"

"Does she bite?"

"She's a movie star. She does whatever she wants. Come with me."

They left the motor home and headed for the wardrobe trailer, where Marisol was being fitted for one of her costumes. They knocked and were ushered inside.

Marisol was standing on a platform, modeling a full-length evening gown. A twenty-something man was instructing two middle-aged women on how to alter the hem of the gown.

Marisol looked at Crow, regarding him with a mixture of curiosity and amusement.

He looked at her impassively. It was difficult to gauge all that he saw, but Jesse knew from experience that he saw everything.

Frankie whispered to the young man, who then clapped his hands. The two women helped Marisol remove the gown. For a brief instant, she stood unself-consciously before her visitors, dressed only in her panties. Then one of the women hastily draped a bathrobe over her shoulders and the three of them left the trailer. Marisol closed the robe and tied the sash.

"Mr. Cromartie," she said.

"Crow," he said.

"What exactly is it that you do, Crow?"

"I provide personal security services."

"Are you good at it?"

Crow didn't say anything.

Marisol moved closer to him.

"I'm concerned about my husband," she said, lowering her voice.

"Concerned how," Crow said.

"We're going through an ugly divorce. He frightens me."

"Is he here in Paradise?"

"Not that I know of."

"But you're frightened of him regardless."

"I am."

"And you want protection."

"Yes."

Crow didn't say anything.

"Are you tough, Mr. Crow," Marisol said.

Crow looked at her.

"Tough enough," he said.

She stepped back.

"He'll do," she said to Frankie.

Crow agreed to start immediately. He insisted on an adjoining room in Marisol's hotel. Frankie promised to do what she could.

After leading Crow to Marisol's trailer, Frankie and Jesse wandered off.

"You were right," she said.

"In what way?"

"He's awesome."

"He'll do."

Frankie laughed.

"Do you have dinner plans," Jesse said.

"I'm up to my neck in work. I'm going to eat at my desk."

"Think how much more fulfilled you'd be were you to engage in an evening of gourmandizing and debauchery."

She looked at him questioningly.

"I can offer you both," he said.

"And you a highly respected officer of the law."

"Only during business hours."

"Okay."

"Okay what?"

"Let the games begin," she said.

26

Ryan reached Jackson Hole, Wyoming, home of Grand Teton National Park, in record time.

Having smoked enough meth to keep him awake and wired, he had driven the nearly eight hundred and fifty miles from Los Angeles in less than thirteen hours.

He had pawned his gold Rolex, the watch that Marisol had given him, for five thousand dollars. He knew he had taken a heavy loss on the deal, but the money would fund his trip and allow him a brief stretch of financial breathing room, as well as enough Shabu to last him for weeks.

The Tetons stop was part of his revenge scheme. His plan called for him to make two phone calls, the first of which was to Marisol. As expected, she didn't answer, so he left a lengthy message informing her that he was preparing to spend ten or so days camping in the Tetons, time spent clearing his mind and cleansing his soul.

The second call was to himself, or, rather, to his cell phone. When it answered, he selected the option that allowed him to change the greeting so that it now informed callers that he was currently camping in the Jackson Hole area and would be out of cell range for a while.

He placed both calls because he wanted them both to appear in his cell-phone records.

At the main gate, he purchased a ticket for entry into the park. It noted his length of stay as two weeks and listed his license plate number.

"Welcome to the Cowboy State," the ranger on duty said, waving him on.

He parked the Prius and got out. He stretched, breathing in the crisp, clean mountain air. He walked along a tree-lined path, deep in thought. He had the uneasy feeling he had overlooked something.

He got back in the car. He reached into the glove compartment and removed the summons. He read it again. Carefully. He knew at once what it was. The insurance policy.

Shortly after their marriage, Marisol had taken out a million-dollar life insurance policy naming Ryan the sole beneficiary. The policy was not mentioned in the summons.

Which meant it was still in full force and effect.

———

Once the sun set and the rangers had gone home, Ryan left the park and headed east, stopping once, at a Holiday Inn near Des Moines.

In the dark, he removed the license plates from a parked Honda and mounted them on his Prius. With so many of these hybrids on the highway, there was now little chance that his would be discovered. He got back on the highway.

One thought kept running through his mind. A million dollars' worth of insurance. With him as the beneficiary.

Damn.

He was gonna be a millionaire.

He pressed harder on the accelerator. He didn't stop until he reached Salem, Massachusetts.

27

On a cold and rainy fall morning, Jesse passed through security and entered the bustling lobby of the Cassidy Building. The wintry weather bothered him because he knew that today was the first day of the Major League Baseball playoffs, and he believed that the chill would hamper the performance of the players.

At the front desk, he told the middle-aged receptionist that he wished to see Richard Cassidy. She regarded him as though she had just caught wind of something rotten.

"Is Mr. Cassidy expecting you," the woman said, her nose raised as if in search of fresh air.

"Metaphorically speaking, yes," Jesse said.

"Excuse me?"

"Would you please tell Mr. Cassidy that Jesse Stone is here to see him."

"Mr. Cassidy doesn't see people without an appointment."

"He'll see me."

"Perhaps I'm not making myself clear. Mr. Cassidy doesn't see anyone without an appointment."

"I'm not here to argue with you, madam. I'm the police chief, and if you refuse to announce me, I'll arrest you and have you hauled off to jail."

The woman stared at Jesse, then picked up the phone and punched in three numbers. She swiveled her chair around so that her back was to him. She cupped the speaker with her hand and spoke quietly.

"There's a Jesse Stone here to see Mr. Cassidy," she said.

Jesse couldn't hear what the party at the other end of the line was saying. He glanced around at the ornate lobby of the brick-and-glass edifice, all angles and curves, architecturally influenced by Frank Gehry. His attention returned to the receptionist.

"I've already told him that, but he's rather insistent," she said into the phone.

After a brief pause, she said, "That's right."

Another pause.

"He did mention that he was the police chief, yes."

She listened.

After a few moments she put the phone down.

She looked at Jesse.

"Take the last elevator on your right to the penthouse floor," she said.

"Sweet," he said.

"You weren't really going to arrest me, right?"

Jesse smiled.

"You'll never know," he said, and headed for the elevator.

The top floor of the Cassidy Building featured floor-to-ceiling windows that offered an exceptional view of Paradise Harbor and the ocean beyond. No sailors had chosen to brave the churning wintry sea, save for a lone commercial schooner bearing a sign that read HARBOR CRUISES.

An attractive woman in her late thirties greeted Jesse as he stepped off the elevator. She was dressed for serious business, in a tailored charcoal-gray suit worn with a slate-blue silk blouse that featured long collar points and pearl buttons. She was all smiles.

"Chief Stone," she said, extending her hand. "I'm Jacqueline Adams, Mr. Cassidy's executive assistant."

Jesse took her hand. Her grip was firm.

"You're very fortunate that Mr. Cassidy could see you now," she said.

"All morning I had this feeling that today was my lucky day," Jesse said.

Her smile flickered for a moment.

"You have no idea how jammed up his schedule usually is," she said.

"And you think my life is easy?"

"No. No. I didn't mean it that way," she said, recovering her smile. "Please follow me."

She led Jesse down a long corridor, past a maze of closed doors and brightly lit conference rooms, to Richard Cassidy's corner suite.

She knocked lightly on the door, and before opening it, she spoke softly to Jesse.

"Can I get you anything? Water? Coffee?"

"Nothing, thank you," he whispered back.

She ushered him inside. The office was immense.

Richard Cassidy stepped from behind his oversized desk. He was dressed casually in a blue blazer, white shirt, and khaki trousers.

He grabbed hold of Jesse's hand and placed an arm around his shoulder as if he were greeting an old and cherished friend. He led Jesse to a sitting area that overlooked the harbor.

"Did Jackie offer you something?" he said. "Coffee? Water?"

"I'm good," Jesse said.

Cassidy nodded to Jacqueline Adams, who closed the door firmly behind her as she left, smiling all the while.

"Please sit down," Cassidy said.

The sitting area comprised a sofa, a love seat, and an over-stuffed armchair, all upholstered in white silk. Spotless, too,

Jesse noticed. Side cabinets and a coffee table completed the array.

Jesse sat on the sofa, and Cassidy sat opposite him on the armchair.

"Nice digs," Jesse said.

"Thank you," Cassidy said. "Construction was completed last fall and we moved in just after the first of the year. We're already being mentioned in the architectural journals."

"How nice for you."

"I've never been prouder of anything in my life."

"Really?"

"Absolutely."

"Does that include your family?"

"I beg your pardon?"

"You said you've never been prouder of anything in your life. Does that include your family?"

"I'm not certain that I appreciate that remark, Chief Stone."

"Jesse."

Cassidy didn't say anything.

"Are you more proud of the building than, say, your daughter?"

"My daughter?"

"Are you proud of Courtney?"

"Of course I'm proud of Courtney."

"She seems to be experiencing some kind of distress."

"She seems to be experiencing some kind of harassment. It appears to us as if you're dogging her."

"If that's what you perceive, Mr. Cassidy, you're mistaken."

"Come off it, Chief Stone. Jesse. She's little more than a child."

"She's a young adult who's acting out some kind of cry for attention."

"Is that your professional opinion?"

"Look, I didn't come here to get into another argument with you. Courtney's in some kind of trouble. And I don't just mean that she broke a few laws. I'd like to see if there's any way I can help her."

"How about you help her by returning to your police station and finding something better to pursue than the harassment of an innocent child."

"You don't really get it, do you?"

"Oh, I get it, all right. I get just what you're about."

Jesse didn't say anything.

"You've got your hand out just like they all do."

"You think this is about extortion?"

Cassidy didn't say anything.

"That's what you think?"

"How much do you want," Cassidy said.

Jesse glared at him.

"Your daughter appears to be careening into some serious trouble," he said. "I'm not altogether convinced that either you or Mrs. Cassidy actually grasps that fact."

Richard Cassidy stood.

"Thank you for your concern, Chief Stone," he said. "Duly

noted and appreciated. Now, if you'll excuse me, there are matters that require my immediate attention."

Jesse stood.

He looked at Richard Cassidy for a few moments.

Then he left.

28

Jesse was sitting at his desk, silently staring out the window, when Molly came in and sat down.

"What's wrong," she said.

"Nothing."

"Come on. Out with it."

Jesse swiveled his chair around and looked at her.

"There's nothing wrong."

Molly didn't say anything.

"Sometimes I think it's not worth it."

"What's not worth it?"

"The job. It's not worth it."

"Feeling sorry for ourselves, are we?"

"Here I'm trying to figure out what can be done to assist this young woman . . . this child, really . . . who might just as well be standing in the middle of the street screaming 'Help me,' and all I get is resistance."

Molly didn't say anything.

"Carter Hansen tells me to leave the girl alone because it's bad for business. Aaron Silver says to lay off because her father is his biggest contributor. And the father tells me to name my price."

"You mean he offered you a bribe?"

"Yes."

"He actually told you to name your price?"

"He did."

"How much did you ask for?"

Jesse looked at her.

"She nearly killed herself," he said.

"What else?"

"That's not enough?"

"There's something else. I know it."

"The water commissioner is accusing me of persecuting him and now won't talk to me."

"William Goodwin thinks you're persecuting him?"

"Yes."

"The little midget?"

"'Little midget' is redundant."

Molly didn't say anything.

"And it's escalating. For the life of me I can't understand why. I'm telling you, Molly, it's not worth it."

"So you are feeling sorry for yourself."

"It's a thankless job."

Molly didn't say anything.

"Exhausting, too."

"Why don't you do what you always do when you're feeling sorry for yourself?"

"What's that?"

"Go home and drink half a bottle of scotch."

"I don't do that anymore."

"So then it's not so bad."

Jesse looked at her.

"Time was all kinds of stuff set you off," she said. "The job. Jenn. Yourself. You're better now."

Jesse shrugged.

"Don't shrug. You are."

"It still makes me crazy."

"This job would make anybody crazy. But you're good at it. You're graced with the rare gift of compassion. You actually care. Which is admirable. And people care about you, Jesse."

"Including you?"

"Especially me."

Jesse smiled.

Molly stood.

"Now, if you don't mind, I'd like to go home and feed my family."

"Thanks, Molly."

"You're a good man, Jesse," she said.

She sauntered out of the office only to turn around in the doorway.

"I knew it," she said.

"Knew what?"

"That it was redundant. Sometimes I just like to amuse myself."

29

It was late afternoon when Jesse parked in front of Ida Fearnley's Craftsman bungalow in the north end of Paradise. Lush mountain laurel and rhododendrons, still green, gave the property an air of seclusion. Elm and maple trees, yellow and red, cast shadows on the lawn.

Jesse lowered the windows of his cruiser and breathed the cool afternoon air. Above, large cirrus clouds hung heavy with the promise of rain.

Ida's Lincoln pulled into her driveway. It took her a few moments to extricate herself from behind the wheel.

She noticed Jesse leaning against his cruiser.

"I think it's time we had a little chat, Ida," Jesse said.

"On or off the record?"

"However you'd like it."

"Off. I suppose you'll be wanting coffee."

"Coffee would be good."

She climbed the steps to her porch and motioned for him to follow as she unlocked the door and opened it.

Inside, they were greeted by two oversized tortoiseshell cats, who wove between Ida's legs as she walked down the hall.

"Sadie. Cybill. Enough," Ida said.

It was only after she poured some dry food into their bowls that they settled down.

Ida fired up the coffeemaker. She took out a box of ladyfingers and placed several on a plate in front of Jesse, who sat at her kitchen table.

"I can't say I'm surprised by your visit," Ida said as she waited for the coffee to brew. "You've certainly managed to upset him."

She poured two cups and brought them to the table. She put them down, then she put herself down, heavily, on the chair across from Jesse. She sighed deeply as she sat.

"What do you know," she said.

Jesse told her.

"He's involved. Both he and Oscar."

Jesse didn't say anything.

"Over the last few years, as he became less and less relevant at the state level, he became more and more militant here. At first it was just the ranting. How many people on the planet go to bed thirsty? Waterborne diseases are the leading cause of death in children under the age of five? You know, stuff like that."

"And?"

"Nobody took him seriously."

"Why, do you suppose?"

"Lots of reasons. He was from a small town. He had no clout. His issues were perceived as politically inconvenient. He visited the state capitol regularly and got nowhere fast. What remains unspoken is that he was the subject of ridicule down there. The way he dressed, his size, his voice … after a day spent being diminished by the Springfield old boys' club, it took him weeks to recover. He told me it was like the schoolyard all over again. Only this time he was being bullied insidiously."

Jesse didn't say anything.

"I think the critical moment came when he made the leaky-pipes proposal. He had personally authorized a study which proved that the pipes carrying fresh water from the Massachusetts reservoirs to the neighborhoods in and around Paradise were old and profusely leaking, costing the state millions of gallons of wasted water. He made a proposal to have those pipes either replaced or repaired. They ignored him. I think that's when he snapped."

"Meaning?"

"What you suspected. He and Oscar worked out a scheme which identified those who they believed were the biggest abusers and then penalized them. When they realized that their scheme had gone undetected, they upped the ante. They went after everyone."

"By falsifying the meter readings."

"Yes."

"How were they able to get away with it?"

"They jacked up the rates in such a way as to make the raises barely noticeable. They started with one percent and, over time, inched closer to three percent. Recently they exceeded it."

"Which may have been the tipping point."

"Perhaps."

"It's when the complaints began."

Ida didn't say anything.

"What did they do with the money?"

"Well, first they repaired the damaged pipes. Then they started to give it away. They made anonymous donations to drought-stricken territories around the world. I don't really know any of the specifics. I heard him mention places like Africa and India. Disaster areas like Haiti and Japan. As I say, I don't really know the details."

They sat quietly, awkwardly, for a time. Jesse sipped his coffee. Ida ate several ladyfingers.

"Why didn't you come forward with this?"

"I don't know, Jesse. I suppose I should have. But I couldn't. He's a visionary. He means everything to me."

Jesse didn't say anything.

"After so many years of working with someone, you grow close. You come to admire him, to believe in him. You never question his values because over time they have also become yours. They were so cruel to him. They couldn't see beyond his appearance. They humiliated him. He'd come back from his meetings so dispirited. It broke my heart."

"So you looked the other way?"

"I guess. At first I didn't know. They met behind closed doors. Oscar was his acolyte. He worshipped the man. William was most likely the first person who ever took him seriously. Oscar would do anything for him."

"Including falsifying records."

Ida didn't say anything.

"When did you learn?"

"The meetings became more frequent. I was being asked to produce past records. Instructed to intercept invoices prior to their being sent. I suppose that's when I really knew. But I couldn't bring myself to admit it."

"When was that?"

"A while ago."

Jesse didn't say anything.

"I guess I'm in trouble," she said.

"I don't know, Ida. This is all so improbable. Have you any sense of the overall size of the thefts?"

"The thefts?"

"That's what they were."

"Yes. I guess I can see that."

"Do you?"

"Do I what?"

"Have any idea of the overall size of the thefts."

"My guess is they were big. Not Madoff big, but significant."

Jesse didn't say anything.

"There is one thing," Ida said.

"What's that?"

"There's been tension between them of late. Ever since you started nosing around."

"Between Oscar and William?"

"Yes."

"Why?"

"It has something to do with money. They've taken to arguing. A lot. Which they never did before."

"Over money?"

"Yes."

Jesse didn't say anything.

"What will happen to him," she said.

"He's likely to be held accountable."

"Does that mean jail time?"

"I'm a cop, Ida, not a judge."

"What are you going to do?"

"I don't know. I need to mull this over for a while."

"He wouldn't do well in jail."

"I know."

"I don't suppose I would, either," she said.

30

How's it going," Jesse said.

"As you might expect," Crow said.

They were drinking coffee alongside the craft service truck, a sort of fast-food place on wheels that provided snacks and between-meals goodies for the movie personnel.

Marisol was in the nearby makeup-and-hair trailer. Crow's attention was totally focused on the people entering and exiting it.

"What's she like?"

"She's very demanding. She wants things her way. She becomes agitated when they're not. On the other hand, she's extremely self-centered."

Jesse didn't say anything.

"I suppose she's not a bad person. It's just that she's preoccu-pied with herself. But she's probably no different from high-profile politicians and corporate bigwigs."

The two men drank their coffee.

"Have I mentioned that she's also an amazing pain in the ass?" Crow said.

"How disillusioning."

"She's never satisfied. Nothing suits her. She complains constantly."

Jesse didn't say anything.

"She's frightened."

"Still?"

"She admitted that she did something she knew would piss him off."

"Dare I ask?"

"She bounced a check on him. Now she's afraid he's in a financial bind and that's why he'll come after her."

"Do you believe it?"

"That he'll come after her?"

"Yes."

"Never take any threat lightly."

The door to the trailer opened, and a middle-aged woman wearing a ball cap and a smock stuck her head out. She looked around until she spotted Crow.

"She wants you," the woman said.

Crow waved to her.

"My turn in the barrel," he said as he headed for the trailer.

"Try not to hurt yourself," Jesse said.

Ryan had rented the cabin through Craigslist and had arranged to pick up the keys at a post office box in Salem. They had been left in the name Buddy Fairbanks.

He drove ten miles to the cabin, located on the outskirts of South Hamilton, a short distance from Paradise, hidden in dense tree cover. It was equipped with a kitchen, satellite dish, and worn but comfortable furniture.

He carried his groceries inside. He dumped his duffel bag in the bedroom. He ate a peanut butter and jelly sandwich, showered, and climbed into bed.

So far, so good, he thought. In more than three days of travel across the width of the United States, no one had seen him. No one knew his whereabouts. He was a ghost.

He rolled over, closed his eyes, and slept.

31

'm not exactly certain why you're here," District Attorney
Aaron Silver said.

He was sitting at his desk, facing Marty Reagan and Jesse,
who were seated opposite him.

"The hearing," Jesse said.

"What about it?"

"It's scheduled?"

"For Thursday," Silver said.

"With Judge Green?"

"Yes."

"Are you planning to recuse yourself," Jesse said.

"Why in the hell would I do that?"

"Because it would be the right thing for you to do."

"You're out of line, Jesse."

Jesse didn't say anything.

"What's with this guy," Silver said to Reagan.

Reagan shrugged.

"We're done here," Silver said, standing.

Jesse remained seated.

"I said we're done."

"If I have to, I'm prepared to scream bloody murder all the way to the Supreme Court."

"What in the fuck is that supposed to mean?"

"Richard Cassidy is one of your biggest campaign contributors. If you don't recuse yourself, you'll be creating one hell of an ethical dilemma for yourself."

"You're questioning my integrity?"

"Come off it, Aaron. Appoint Marty to stand in your stead and get the fuck out of the way."

Silver didn't say anything.

"And while you're at it, take Judge Green with you."

"You're off your rocker, Jesse, you know that," Silver said.

"Everyone knows you two are joined at the hip. She's your go-to judge. Get her to recuse herself, too. Don't stink this up, Aaron."

"You are one piece of business coming in here and talking to me this way."

"So you'll do it?"

Silver was silent. He swiveled his chair around and stared out the window for a while.

Jesse glanced at Reagan, who briefly made eye contact with him before looking away.

"All right," Silver said, his back still turned to Jesse.

"Wise choice," Jesse said, standing.

"Get the fuck out of here, Jesse," Silver said.

Jesse said nothing as he left.

So tomorrow you start shooting," Jesse said. "Are you nervous?"

"Opening-night jitters," Frankie said.

"What could go wrong?"

"Most likely nothing."

"So what are you nervous about?"

"Comes with the territory."

They were sitting on Jesse's porch, having just eaten an extra-large meatball, garlic, and onion pizza, which they washed down with Sam Adams ale.

The sun was bouncing its last rays of the day off the restless waters of the bay. Crickets had begun to chirp their night songs. The fall air was brisk, absent humidity. It smelled of the sea and the encroaching chill of winter.

They were sitting together on Jesse's love seat, separated only by Mildred Memory, who had insinuated herself between them.

"This is nice," Frankie said. "Almost makes me forget why I'm here."

"The reason you're here is to overeat, suffer unspeakable bouts of lassitude, then recover in time to engage in super-human feats of gymnastic-style lovemaking."

"I knew that."

"What time tomorrow do you start?"

"First shot should be off by six-thirty."

"In the morning?"

She looked up at him.

He looked at his watch.

"My God," he said. "We'd better speed through this lassitude part."

"If only there hadn't been meatballs," she said.

"It's always something."

She looked up at him. She inadvertently dislodged Mildred when she put her arms around Jesse's neck and pulled him to her.

"This is great fun," she said just before she kissed him.

32

The first day of shooting generally sets the tone for the entire movie.

Everyone on the set takes special note of how well the director interacts with the actors, the cinematographer, the crew, and the staff. The quality of that communication sends out signals as to whether or not the production will prove to be smooth sailing or rough going.

"If the fish stinks from the head," Frankie said, "people will smell it almost immediately."

Standing alongside Carter Hansen and a handful of other local dignitaries who were also watching the proceedings, Jesse realized anew how tedious the process of filmmaking actually was.

Frankie had described what was taking place as a tracking shot. The camera was mounted on a wheeled dolly that was pulled rapidly backward along a specially constructed section of what resembled train track. The moving dolly would precede the action, allowing the camera to photograph the scene from in front of it, all the while moving rapidly apace with it.

They were rehearsing the first scene. A young camera assistant stood beside the dolly mount and placed the clapper board directly in front of the camera. It displayed the title of the film, the name of the director, the scene number, and the time of day.

"*A Taste of Arsenic*, scene one, rehearsal," the assistant shouted. Then he slammed the top of the clapper board onto its base.

"Action," called the director.

Marisol burst through the front door of a large office building, then stopped. She looked around. She reached into her purse and pulled out a cell phone. She looked at it, then she looked up. A thought registered in her eyes. She walked hurriedly toward a car that was parked in front of the building. When she reached it, she opened the driver's-side door and got in.

The director yelled, "Cut."

"That's a cut," the assistant director called out. "Reset. Everyone back to first positions."

People returned to their original places and prepared for another take.

While this was going on, Jesse spotted Crow approaching Marisol, accompanied by a little girl, who looked to be about seven or eight, and an older woman, most likely the girl's mother.

He watched as Crow introduced the girl to Marisol, who stood beside her while the mother photographed the two of them together. The child, all smiles, shook hands with Marisol, then she and her mother hurried away.

After a few moments, Jesse saw Marisol turn to Crow in a rage. Everyone present could hear what she was saying.

"How dare you bring strangers to me when I'm acting," Marisol said to him. "You ruined the shot."

"The child played hooky in order to see you," Crow said.

"She destroyed my concentration."

"Well, if it makes any difference, you have a fan for life."

"Tell her to get in line."

Marisol stormed away in the direction of her motor home.

She turned back to Crow.

"That was truly stupid," she said. "Never again. Don't ever interrupt me like that again. You hear me?"

Crow didn't say anything.

"Do you understand?"

He nodded.

She stepped inside the motor home and slammed the door behind her.

Everyone on the set pretended that what they had just witnessed hadn't occurred. They turned their attention elsewhere and went on with their work.

Frankie Greenberg made her way toward Marisol's trailer, stopping only to have a word with Crow.

"I'm sorry," she said to him. "First day is always the toughest. Can you forgive her?"

He grunted.

"Please," Frankie said. "I promise to make it up to you."

Then she turned and walked quickly to the motor home. She knocked on the door and went inside.

Jesse meandered over to where Crow was standing.

"That went well," he said.

Crow didn't say anything.

"Kid freaked her out," Jesse said.

"Nah. She was looking for an excuse."

"An excuse?"

"To remind people that she's the star."

"She needed to do that?"

"You can lay odds that no one will forget what just went down, and they'll pussyfoot around her for the rest of the shoot."

"So why did she storm off?"

"For effect."

"You mean she wasn't upset?"

"No."

"How do you know?"

"She does everything for effect."

"Isn't that a cynical opinion," Jesse said.

"Cynicism is what floats my boat."

"So you're not thinking of quitting."

Crow looked at him.

"What, and give up show business," he said.

R yan Rooney left the cabin in the late afternoon and drove to Paradise. It was easy to find the convoy of movie vehicles in such a small town.

Arriving at the end of the day, amid the hubbub of wrap time, would more easily allow him to accomplish what he intended to do. He parked and headed for the base camp.

Ryan watched as the various departments packed up their equipment and began loading it into their respective vehicles. Everybody was on the move, which gave him his opening.

Unrecognizable in a blond wig, dark glasses, and full beard, Ryan headed for the three-banger that housed the assistant directors' cubicle.

A three-banger is a twenty-foot trailer that has been subdivided into three separate rooms. In addition to the ADs' office, it also housed a holding section for the extras and an individual dressing room for a member of the supporting cast.

As he expected, no one was in the ADs' section.

At wrap, each of the assistant directors is busy with the distribution of the call sheets and maps for the next day's shoot, as well as providing information about where the various departments could watch the screening of the rushes, the raw footage of that day's work.

Ryan slipped inside the trailer and quickly gathered copies of all the production schedules and contact sheets. The schedules detailed every day's workload and its location. The contact sheets listed the local addresses of everyone connected with the movie.

He also grabbed a copy of the script.

No one noticed him. And then he was gone.

He stopped at a Star Time Grocery and bought himself a frozen pizza and a six-pack of Rolling Rock. He splurged and also bought a pint of Ben & Jerry's Cherry Garcia ice cream.

Then he returned to the cabin.

33

Portia Cassidy emerged from the Paradise Mall loaded with packages, heading for her car, where she was surprised to find Jesse Stone. He was leaning against the right-front fender of his cruiser, which was parked beside her BMW roadster. His face was turned to the sun.

Portia loaded her packages into the BMW without acknowledging him.

"I'm working on my tan," Jesse said.

"Why? Surely there must be any number of adolescent miscreants you could be dogging," Portia said.

"You know what I'm sorry about?"

"Should I care?"

"I'm sorry we got off to such a bad start."

"Spare me."

"No. I mean it. You see, I think we might have some common ground."

Portia now stood beside the car, facing him.

"I'm going to regret asking, aren't I," she said.

Jesse looked at her.

"I think Courtney could use our help," he said.

"Our help."

"That's funny. Your husband said the same thing. Is it so outlandish to think that I might want to help get to the bottom of what's causing her to behave as she is."

"Yes."

"Yes what?"

"Yes, it's outlandish."

"Come on, Portia. You believe I'm an overzealous policeman, and I believe you're a vindictive mother. Okay. So be it. But can't we both step out of character for a moment and just talk to each other?"

Portia didn't say anything.

"We've both got a problem here. Mine is dealing with an unrepentant lawbreaker with issues. Yours is trying to get to the bottom of your daughter's behavior."

"That's how you perceive this?"

"Yes."

"Look," she said. "Even if I were to appreciate your point of view, which I don't, by the way, I would still maintain that what's happening with Courtney is none of your business. You don't know her. You don't know us. You don't know anything. So for the sake of this conversation, allow me to advise you to, how shall I put it, stay the fuck out of it."

"I'm sorry you feel that way."

"Well, I do."

"It doesn't have to be like this."

"Once again you're wrong. Listen to me, Jesse. I'll say this once and then we're going to act like it never happened. We are the Cassidys. We don't seek your opinion as to how we live our lives or conduct our family business. We buy and sell you. You don't count. Do I make myself clear?"

Jesse sighed.

"Now, if you'll please step away from my car," she said.

Jesse did.

She got into it. She lowered her window.

"Thanks for your time," she said. "I know how valuable it is."

She gunned the engine, pulled out, and sped away.

34

Crow noticed the man the moment he and Marisol stepped outside of Daisy's, where they had gone for a quick supper.

It was just after nine o'clock on a chilly weeknight, and the restaurant crowd had thinned considerably. Marisol's driver was parked in front, waiting for them.

The man was standing across the street, along with four others, all of them in their thirties, all drinking beer from cans. The man was wearing a porkpie hat, loose jeans, and a wiseguy expression on his pockmarked face. When he spotted Marisol, he grinned broadly and headed in her direction.

"Hey, look," he said to his friends. "It's a real live movie star."

Crow motioned for Marisol to stand behind him.

The man approached them, followed closely by his four companions. He stopped just shy of where Crow was standing.

"Move over, old man," he said. "I wanna get me a good look at this here movie star."

Crow didn't say anything.

He was totally calm.

The man moved a couple of steps closer.

"What are you, hard of hearing," he said. "Get the fuck out of my way."

With barely a glance at him, Crow hit the man with the edge of his right hand, above the upper lip and just below his nose.

The man screamed.

He went down, doubled up on the ground, his face buried in his hands.

Crow's move was so explosive that before the others could even react, he had a gun in his hand, pointed at them.

"Please don't tempt me," Crow said.

The man in the porkpie hat lay on the ground, moaning. The others stopped dead in their tracks.

Crow took Marisol's hand and guided her to the waiting vehicle. He helped her inside.

He took one last look at the five men and then got in the car.

The driver pulled into traffic and sped away.

Marisol sat in the corner of the backseat, staring at Crow.

"My God," she said.

Crow returned the gun to his shoulder holster.

He didn't say anything.

35

R yan pored over the production schedule. It was day seven that caught his eye, the first day of the second week of the shoot.

Weather permitting, the unit was scheduled to set up shop along the west coast of Paradise Inlet.

A number of small cottages dotted the coastline. Most were rudimentary, built years ago as summer places for vacationers. Many of them were without heat or insulation.

When the long summer days shortened into early fall, many of the occupants closed up their cottages for the season. *A Taste of Arsenic* was scheduled to shoot in one of them for two successive nights.

———

Ryan drove slowly, checking out the landscape. He spotted the movie people almost immediately.

A handful of cars and a couple of oversized trucks were parked in front of a two-story cottage. A paint crew was sprucing it up while the art department staff was off-loading furniture. Landscapers were installing squares of new grass on the front lawn.

Scaffolding was being constructed in front of the cottage to hold the large lighting units that would illuminate the night, as well as the generators required to power them.

Ryan continued his drive along the inlet. He could see that many of the cottages had been closed down. There was very little activity in most of them. Few if any cars were parked in the driveways.

He doubled back and spotted an empty cottage two doors away from the shooting location.

"That's the one," he said to himself.

Later that night, Ryan returned to Fisherman's Road. The crew had all left.

Driving with his lights off, Ryan pulled his Prius into the driveway of the cottage he had spotted earlier. He parked in back.

The night sky was cloudless, and the sliver of moon provided just enough light.

He paced the exterior of the house, looking for a way in. He saw no security system. He stepped onto the back porch and tried to open the kitchen window. It was locked.

He picked up a rock and smashed one of the window's six glass panes. He lifted out the jagged ends, reached inside, and unlocked the window. Then he raised it and climbed through to the kitchen.

The adjacent dining room was furnished with an old wooden table and four chairs, as well as a serving hutch and a crockery-filled cabinet.

The living room was larger. A worn sofa and love seat were its main furnishings, along with a pair of wicker chairs and a couple of mismatched side tables.

Ryan wandered down the hall to the bedrooms. The larger of the two had a queen-size bed with a night table on each side. The smaller had a pair of single beds separated by a dresser. There was one bathroom with a sink and a combination bathtub/shower.

For Ryan's purposes, it was perfect.

36

Jesse arrived early for the hearing. He was sitting in Judge Emanuel Weissberg's outer office, chatting with Marty Reagan, when the Cassidy family stormed in.

Upon seeing Reagan, Richard Cassidy approached him.

"Where's Aaron," he said.

"Not here."

"Why not?"

"He recused himself."

Cassidy gazed at his wife, Portia, who stared daggers at him.

Courtney stood between them.

"He can't do that," Portia said.

Reagan shrugged.

"Why aren't we in Judge Green's chambers," Richard said.

"She recused herself as well."

"What in the hell's going on here," Portia said.

"Nothing out of the ordinary," Reagan said. "I'll be representing the DA's office."

Portia stepped over to her husband and spoke just loudly enough for everyone to hear.

"We're being fucked," she said.

"No, we're not. Something probably came up."

"You're such a fool, Richard. Nothing came up. He bailed on us is what happened. And after all we've done for him. It makes me sick."

Richard shook his head. She glared at him. The room became icily silent.

Portia sat down, picked up a magazine, and thumbed sightlessly through it. Courtney opened her bag, removed her cell phone, and started texting. Richard paced.

The door opened, and Judge Weissberg appeared. He was thin and scholarly-looking, wearing black-framed eyeglasses and bearing a ramrod-straight posture. With a wave, he led them into his chambers, where they all found seats. The room was small and cramped with so many bodies crowded in.

"I am Emanuel Weissberg," he said. "I'll be conducting this hearing. That is, unless there are any objections."

"It was my impression that Judge Green would be conducting the hearing," Portia said.

"You were mistaken," Judge Weissberg said.

She shifted uneasily under his steely gaze. She was suddenly alert to the possibility that she might have offended him. She looked away.

"If there's nothing else," Weissberg said, "let's begin. Mr. Reagan?"

"Good morning, Your Honor," Marty Reagan said.

He introduced the participants and reviewed the charges against Courtney. He informed the judge that the Commonwealth would be seeking a one-year suspension of her driving privileges, as per the law. He proposed that she be placed under probation for a similar period of time. He also asked that she be given an equal period of community service.

"Does the defendant have anything to say for herself," the judge said.

Courtney shrugged.

"May I speak on her behalf, Your Honor," Richard said.

"You may," Judge Weissberg said. "So long as you're brief."

"I'll do my best, Your Honor," Richard said, standing. "As you can see, my daughter is a teenager whose actions were most certainly misguided. She is extremely apologetic and remorseful. She's seventeen years old, Your Honor. The penalties that the Commonwealth is seeking seem unnecessarily harsh. We ask that she be remanded to the custody of both her mother and me without being further restricted."

He sat down.

"Is it true she was a repeat offender? Weren't there three incidents? One of them involving a serious accident?"

Richard stood again.

"We acknowledge that the accident was indeed her fault. We made restitution to the driver, who has declined to press charges. It's possible that on the other two occasions, she may have been the victim of entrapment."

"Entrapment?"

"She was being unreasonably dogged by a law officer who appears to bear her malice."

"That's a heady charge, Mr. Cassidy," Judge Weissberg said.

Then, acknowledging Jesse's presence, he said, "Is this the law officer?"

"It is," Richard said.

"Chief Stone, is it?"

"Yes, Your Honor," Jesse said.

"What's this all about?"

Jesse stood.

"I witnessed the accident," he said. "Ms. Cassidy was texting on her cell phone when she ran a stop sign and broadsided another vehicle. Afterward, she exhibited disdain for what she referred to as a 'stupid law' and expressed her opinions to me in an argumentative and disrespectful manner."

"May I raise an objection," Portia said.

"No," the judge said. "Go on, Chief Stone."

"When I saw that Ms. Cassidy was unrepentant, I decided to keep an eye on her. I suspected she might be a chronic offender."

"And?"

"On successive days I witnessed her talking on her cell phone while driving. The first time I saw her, I pulled her over and cited her. Once again, she was sullen and argumentative. The next day I caught her doing it again."

Jesse sat down.

"He was badgering her," Portia said.

The judge turned his attention to her.

"Did your daughter actually break the law in the manner Chief Stone has described?"

"You mean was she talking on her cell phone?"

"And texting."

"I have no idea. I sincerely doubt it."

"You're suggesting that Chief Stone is lying," the judge said.

"It's not out of the question. I believe he was out to get her."

Marty Reagan asked for permission to speak.

"In each instance," he said, "Chief Stone impounded the cell phone which Ms. Cassidy had been using. Research proves that each of the phones was engaged at the time of the alleged offense."

"Thank you, Mr. Reagan," the judge said.

He then turned to Portia.

"I'm going to refrain from citing you for contempt, Mrs. Cassidy," he said. "However, one more outburst and I'll have you removed from my chambers and taken into custody. Are we clear about that?"

Portia lowered her eyes.

"Answer me."

"Yes," she said.

"'Yes, Your Honor,'" the judge said. "You'll damn well show respect for this court."

"Yes, Your Honor."

"And I'll hear your apology to Chief Stone."

"Excuse me."

"Apologize to Chief Stone for your insolence."

Portia looked at Jesse.

"I apologize," she said.

"Speak up," the judge said.

"I apologize, Your Honor," she said.

"To Chief Stone," the judge said.

Portia looked at Jesse.

"I apologize, Chief Stone," she said.

Jesse didn't say anything.

The judge sat silently for several moments. Then he addressed Courtney.

"Miss Cassidy," he said. "This court cannot emphasize strongly enough the dangers of distracted driving. Your actions suggest you don't have much regard for that concept. Well, young lady, you're dead wrong. I am herewith revoking your driving privileges for a period of not less than six months. At the end of that term, we'll review the situation in order to determine whether or not I will extend the revocation for an additional six months. I am also sentencing you to six months of community service. The district attorney's office has asked that your service be performed at the Paradise police station, under the supervision of Chief Stone. You will report to him not later than nine a.m. once a week for a period of six months. I will further consider the request for probation and inform the assistant district attorney of my decision."

Judge Weissberg looked directly at each of the Cassidys.

Then he picked up his gavel and slammed it as hard as he could onto a wooden block, which resounded like a gunshot and startled everyone in the room.

"Dismissed," he said.

37

Jesse lagged behind the Cassidys as they left the courthouse. Richard and Portia were clearly agitated. Courtney seemed stunned.

They headed toward a black Lincoln Town Car that was waiting for them at curbside. A driver opened the back door.

"I suppose you're satisfied," Portia said to her husband.

He didn't say anything.

"We got shafted. I certainly hope you're planning to withdraw your support from his reelection campaign."

Richard remained silent.

"Well," Portia said.

She looked at him.

They were now standing beside the Lincoln. The driver

stood awkwardly next to them, holding on to the car door as if for ballast.

Courtney stood apart, shifting her weight from foot to foot, her eyes downcast. She didn't look at either of her parents.

"How dare he abandon us like that," Portia said. "Who contributed more than we did."

"He must have come under some kind of scrutiny," Richard said.

"Probably from someone who has an ax to grind with you."

"Why don't you stay out of it, Portia. You don't know what you're talking about."

"Oh? Now I don't know what I'm talking about."

"Keep out of it."

"To hell with you, Richard."

"Most likely he couldn't risk being compromised," he said, as if to himself.

"So she has to pay the price," Portia said, indicating Courtney.

"I don't mind," Courtney said, looking up at her parents at last.

"What," Portia said.

"Please stop arguing. I'll do what the judge said. I can't stand this constant arguing."

"We're only looking out for your best interests," Richard said.

"You're not. You're making me the scapegoat so that the two of you can continue to fight with each other."

Neither of her parents said anything.

"You hate each other."

"How dare you say a thing like that," Portia said.

"It's true. You hate him. You never say anything nice to him. You're horrible."

"Don't talk to your mother that way," Richard said.

"You're no better than she is," Courtney said.

"Get in the car," Portia said.

"No."

"Do you want to be grounded?"

"I'm as good as grounded already. What does it matter?"

Portia walked over to Courtney and angrily grabbed her arm. "I said get in the car."

"Fuck you," Courtney said, breaking free of Portia's grasp.

Portia slapped her.

Courtney reached for her face, fighting back tears.

Richard stepped between them.

"Do as your mother says. Get in the car."

"Fuck you, too," she said.

She stepped to the car and opened the front passenger-side door. She looked at her parents with contempt.

"You don't know anything," she said.

She got in the car and slammed the door behind her.

Richard and Portia exchanged angry glances. They climbed into the backseat. The driver closed the door after them, quickly got into the car, and drove away.

Jesse stepped from the courthouse shadows. He watched the Lincoln disappear into the late-morning traffic.

When it was out of sight, he got in his cruiser and drove off.

38

The mood on the set was euphoric. The first week had gone smoothly, and the production was both on schedule and on budget.

More important, the rushes had shown Marisol to be delivering the most complex and fully realized performance of her career. Although it was still early in the process, expectation levels for the movie were on the rise.

The Hollywood-based studio executive who was overseeing the production had phoned Marisol to offer his compliments and to schmooze with her.

"Marisol," said the voice on the other end of the line, "it's Ross Danielson."

"Ross," she said. "What a lovely surprise."

"I just had to pick up the phone and tell you how amazing the dailies are."

"Really?"

"You know what a fan of yours I am," he said. "I've never seen you better."

"Oh, Ross. That's so sweet of you."

"I totally mean it. I'm already smelling Oscar."

Marisol giggled.

"I totally mean it. I've mentioned it to Sumner, and he's instructed me to start formulating a campaign."

"An Oscar campaign?"

"Absolutely."

"I don't know what to say."

"Just keep up the good work. Bonnie Garvin in marketing and I are trying to clear our schedules so that we can fly out to see you."

"You mean visit the set?"

"I do."

"Wow."

"I'll let you know," he said.

Fresh flowers sent from the head of the studio appeared in her motor home. Elaborate gift baskets filled with fine wines, fresh fruit, and exotic cheeses showed up in her hotel room.

Frankie had asked Jesse to stop by at lunchtime, and they were seated together in the catering tent when Marisol poked her head in. She sat down with them, accompanied by Crow.

"I heard you were on set," she said to Jesse. "I wanted to stop by and say hello."

Jesse smiled at her.

"I can't thank you enough," Marisol said. "Mr. Crow here has looked after me very well."

Jesse looked at Crow, whose flat-eyed expression revealed nothing.

"Your lovely phone has worked miracles," she said. "Not a single call from him. I can't tell you how relieved I am."

"Which shows in the work," Frankie said. "Things are going extremely well."

"I'm very pleased to hear that," Jesse said.

"We owe you, Jesse," Marisol said.

"Not at all," he said.

She stood.

"I just wanted to stop by and say hello," she said to Jesse. Then she turned to Crow.

"Mr. Crow," she said. "I think I have just enough time for a quick nap."

She smiled and headed for the exit.

Crow stood. He looked briefly at Jesse.

"Mr. Crow," Jesse said.

"I'd appreciate it if you would call me that, too," Crow said.

Then he hurried over to Marisol and accompanied her out of the tent.

"She's happy," Frankie said.

"Seems that way."

"She hasn't heard from him all week. She told me he's gone camping."

Jesse didn't say anything.

"She said that Crow made her feel safe."

"He tends to do that."

Frankie looked at her watch.

"We're almost back. I have to go speak with the First AD."

They stood, and Jesse walked with her to the AD trailer.

"I'm sorry I've been so preoccupied," Frankie said.

"I understand."

"I'll call you."

She kissed him lightly and then disappeared into the trailer.

39

Ryan waited until dark before returning to the cottage. It was Sunday, and the movie company would be at rest until tomorrow.

He drove by the shooting location and saw only a single vehicle parked in front of it. He assumed it belonged to the security officer assigned to look after the equipment, who had more than likely made himself comfortable inside.

Ryan continued past the cottage.

Once out of sight, he turned the Prius around, driving past the location until he reached the cottage closest to the intersection of Lakeside Drive and Fisherman's Road. This cottage, too, had been closed up for the winter.

He turned into the driveway and headed for the back. Once

there, he got out of the car and walked to the detached garage. He pulled on a pair of rubber gloves, jimmied the lock, and opened the door. He backed the Prius inside. He reached for his backpack and closed the garage door behind him.

Using the cottages on his side of the road as cover, he made his way past the location, stopping across the way from the cottage he had chosen. When he was certain that no one was watching, he ran across the road.

He walked to the rear of the cottage and opened the kitchen door, which he had earlier left unlocked.

Once inside, he emptied his backpack. He had brought a two-day supply of food, which he placed in a kitchen cabinet.

Then he went to the smaller of the two bedrooms, where he unloaded the rest of his things.

He picked up his .38-caliber Beretta automatic pistol and press-checked it. He placed it on the night table.

He looked at his watch. It was three-fifteen a.m. He yawned.

He lay down and made himself comfortable.

He couldn't wait to see the look on her face when he pulled the trigger.

40

When Courtney came out of the main building of the Wilburforce School, she was surprised by the sight of Jesse Stone standing beside his cruiser.

"What are you doing," she said to him.

"Working on my tan."

"No. I mean what are you doing here?"

Jesse looked at her.

"Waiting for you."

"I didn't do anything wrong."

"I know."

"So why are you waiting for me?"

"What did you think of the hearing?"

"I think I was railroaded."

" 'Railroaded'?"

"Yes."

"Do you even know what the word means?"

"I was dealt with unfairly."

"It was your mother, right?"

"My mother what?"

"Who used the word."

Courtney didn't say anything.

"I guess the arrogance is hereditary."

"What's that supposed to mean?"

"You weren't railroaded, Courtney. No one was out to get you."

She shifted uncomfortably.

"The first thing that has to happen, if you're going to learn anything from this, is that you have to accept responsibility for what you did."

Jesse moved away from his car and stood face-to-face with her.

"You made a mistake. Several of them. But what's done is done. Now you have to admit those mistakes and take responsibility for them."

"Why are you hassling me this way? Isn't it enough that you made me lose my license, and now I have to walk everywhere? That I have to endure six months of some stupid community service?"

Jesse didn't say anything.

"Why are you so exasperating," Courtney said.

"It's time for you to learn that you're not acting in your own best interests."

"I don't have to listen to this crap." She turned away from him.

"You'd do yourself a favor if you took what I'm saying seriously," he said. "You can't help yourself if you don't first recognize that you need help."

Courtney started to walk away. Over her shoulder, she called back to him.

"Screw you," she said.

"My point exactly," he said.

41

t was early Monday evening when Jesse pulled up in front
of the Community Services Building. He made his way to
William Goodwin's office.

Ida Fearnley greeted him warily.

"He's waiting," she said.

She ushered him inside, where he found Goodwin standing
at his desk. Beside him stood Oscar LaBrea, pointing a short-
barreled Ruger .45-millimeter automatic pistol at Jesse.

Ida remained in the room, closing the door behind her and
leaning against it.

"Aw, hell," Jesse said.

"In case you're wondering, I know how to use it," Oscar said.
"Put your gun on the commissioner's desk."

Jesse sighed.

He took the Colt from his shoulder holster, turned it so that the handle was facing Goodwin, and placed it on the desk. Then he sat down.

"What's this about," he said.

"You've flown too close to the flame," Goodwin said.

"Quit talking in metaphor."

"Are you aware of what the people of Massachusetts are getting away with? Have you any idea how much they're receiving for so little?"

Jesse didn't say anything.

"People are being given the bargain of their lives, and they neither appreciate nor respect it. I tried for years to get them to listen. No one cared. As a result, we continue to squander our most important natural resource. Every time someone takes a piss and flushes the toilet, one and a half gallons of clean water flushes away with it. What's wrong with this picture?"

He began to pace the room. His already high-pitched voice continued to rise with his anxiety level.

"This despicable behavior has to stop."

Goodwin sat down, weary from the energy expended on his diatribe.

"Unbeknownst to them, however, the citizens of Paradise have been personally funding the water facilities of the disenfranchised. Thanks to our efforts," Goodwin said, with a nod to Oscar and Ida, "hundreds of thousands of dollars have been anonymously contributed to help cure the world's water ills. We are singlehandedly changing the planet, drop by drop."

"Illegally," Jesse said.

"What?"

"Regardless of whatever good you think you may be doing, you're breaking the law. You'll be held accountable for it."

"Accountable to whom," Goodwin said.

"To the citizens of Paradise."

"Who's going to tell them?"

"I am," Jesse said.

"That's where you're mistaken," LaBrea said, stepping closer to Jesse. "You won't be alive to tell them."

Jesse turned to LaBrea, whose pistol was still trained on him.

"I'm going to shoot you, you bastard," LaBrea said.

42

The second week of filming was devoted entirely to night work.

The crew had been called for the late afternoon and had completed their prep by sunset. Now they waited for darkness to fall.

At magic hour, those final moments of the good natural light of day, the cast and crew were on set, blocking the scene they were about to shoot. The scene took place on the back porch of the cottage.

As night began its slow descent, bringing with it wisps of cloud and a hint of fog, the director rehearsed the actors, placing them in the various positions that the scene required.

The cinematographer stood alongside the director, noting the actors' movements during the rehearsal.

A camera assistant placed different-colored strips of masking tape on the floor, to indicate the marks the individual actors would need to hit during the scene.

Other crew members delivered props to the set, hung and focused lights, and laid dolly track for the smooth movement of the camera mount. Wardrobe personnel carried costumes and accessories.

Craft service employees brought trays of sandwiches and beverages to a specially laid table located within easy access of the set. Bowls filled with fruit and plates full of cakes and cookies were already on the table. As were jars filled with candy. This allowed members of the cast and crew to grab a snack or a drink without having to venture far from the action.

A group of extras stood at the ready, waiting to be selected by one of the assistant directors for inclusion in the background activity of the scene. Extras were hired by the day, depending on the dictates of the screenplay.

As this was a night shoot, the number of extras was held to a minimum. On this night, only eight of them were in attendance. Later in the evening, when the action moved to the front of the house, they would be called on to appear either on the street or in passing vehicles. As of now, they were gathered near the set, watching the proceedings.

Unnoticed by cast and crew in his beard and wig was Ryan Rooney. He had left the commandeered cottage at nightfall, emboldened by the pipeful of Shabu he had smoked.

He felt great. He felt strong. He was ready.

He walked with purpose to the set. In the organized chaos of working in partial darkness, nobody paid him any mind.

He stood within sight of Marisol, but for all intents and purposes, he was invisible.

Ryan watched as the director finished blocking the scene.

He saw Marisol being accompanied to the makeup trailer by a large man who appeared to be Native American. The man seemed fit, and his movements were lithe and economical. Ryan presumed he was either her assistant or her bodyguard. Or both.

He waited.

She emerged from the makeup truck in the company of the Indian and went to her personal trailer, which was parked a few feet from the set.

He waited.

She soon emerged, in costume and full makeup, ready for work. The Indian led her to the set and the nearby row of canvas-backed director's chairs. One of them had her name embroidered on it.

Marisol sat in her chair and was soon joined by another woman, who Ryan recognized as Frankie Greenberg, whom he remembered from *Tomorrow We Love*.

She sat down next to Marisol, a leather-bound script in her hand.

It was dark, and when Frankie opened her script and turned

to a specific page, she held a flashlight over it. Marisol studied the page, the two women chatting quietly.

Ryan noticed Marisol signaling to the Indian, pointing to Frankie's script and shrugging her shoulders as if to suggest that she wanted her own copy.

The Indian nodded his understanding and stepped over to Marisol's nearby trailer.

He stopped for a moment before going inside. He looked around. Seeing nothing out of the ordinary, he opened the door to the trailer and went inside.

Ryan pulled the .38 from his pocket and quickly moved to where the two women were sitting.

Marisol looked up as he approached, no recognition in her eyes. Then she knew.

"Oh my God," she said.

That was when Ryan shot her.

Frankie stood and started toward him.

That was when he shot her.

Ryan immediately put the gun in his pocket and walked into the darkness.

Unnoticed amid the chaos that followed, he headed for his Prius.

He opened the garage door and got into the car. He removed his wig and placed it under the seat. He engaged the hybrid's silent battery and drove slowly down the driveway.

He turned onto Lakeside Drive, then onto Fisherman's Road.

Then he vanished into the night.

43

The sound of Jesse's cell phone broke the tension in Goodwin's office. He reached into his pocket and pulled out the phone.

"What's up, Molly," he said.

There was a pause before he responded.

"Send everyone you have. Seal it off. Call Captain Healy. I'm on my way," he said, and closed the phone.

Jesse looked up at Goodwin and LaBrea without really seeing them.

"There's been a shooting," he said, almost to himself.

He looked at LaBrea and, without warning, slapped the Ruger from his hand. He reached into his jacket pocket for his .38-caliber Smith & Wesson backup pistol and trained it on a cringing LaBrea.

"Didn't anyone ever tell you that it's bad manners to point guns at people," Jesse said, grabbing LaBrea by the neck.

He smashed the heel of the Smith & Wesson into LaBrea's nose, then let go of him. LaBrea fell heavily to the floor, screaming in pain.

Jesse pocketed LaBrea's gun, then took his Colt from Goodwin's desk and returned it to its holster.

LaBrea's nose was bleeding profusely. Goodwin rushed to his aid.

As Jesse headed for the door, he said to Ida, "Don't wait too long before calling nine-one-one. You wouldn't want him to bleed out."

Jesse stopped in front of the cottage on Lakeside Drive and switched off his siren and lights. He got out of the cruiser.

People were milling about in stunned silence. Some were crying. Others were staring aimlessly into space.

Suitcase hurried over to him.

"Marisol took one shot to the head," he said. "Death was instantaneous. Not pretty."

"Frankie?"

"She was hit in the chest. Bullet did some damage, but it

missed her heart. Medics were noncommittal. Ambulance took her to Paradise General."

"Any idea as to the identity of the shooter?"

"None. No one saw him."

"His whereabouts?"

"Ditto."

"Crow?"

"With the body."

The night sky was lit up by four giant ten-K movie lamps that threw pools of illumination onto the darkened landscape, creating areas of both light and dark.

Jesse saw Crow sitting next to Marisol's covered body. He sat dejectedly amid the circles of light and dark, an eerie portrait of sadness and isolation.

When he saw Jesse and Suitcase approaching, Crow looked up at them.

"This is all on me," he said.

"Tell me how it went down," Jesse said.

"They were waiting to get off the first shot. Frankie was showing her some script changes. I was hovering as usual. She asked me to get her script. It was in the trailer right over there. Inches away. Nothing seemed out of the ordinary, so I went to get it for her. I couldn't have been gone for more than a minute."

"That's when it happened?"

"Guy came out of nowhere and shot them both."

"Any idea who it was?"

"Had to have been the husband."

Jesse didn't say anything.

"Had to have been," Crow said.

Jesse turned to Suitcase.

"Who's here," he said.

"Bauer. Perkins."

"Would you mind finding them and bringing them to me."

"No problem," Suitcase said, and hurried off.

"On my watch," Crow said to Jesse after Suitcase had left. "It was the only time she had been alone since I got here."

"How bad was Frankie?"

"Bad enough."

"She gonna make it?"

"She lost a lot of blood. I was able to stanch it somewhat. She was unconscious when the medics got to her."

"What a mess," Jesse said.

"He won't get away with it. I'll find him."

"He could be halfway to the moon by now."

"I'll find him."

Jesse saw Peter Perkins and Rich Bauer heading in his direction, followed closely by Suitcase.

Jesse stepped away from Crow and took the three officers aside.

"What can we do, Jesse," Suitcase said.

"I want you to phone California DMV and find out what vehicle or vehicles are registered to Ryan Rooney. I need license plate and registration numbers. Then put out an APB. He's likely on the move."

"Got it, Jesse," Suitcase said.

"Pete," Jesse said. "I want you to find phone numbers for Mr. Rooney. Home, cell, everything. Call him. If he answers, bring me the phone. If his machine answers, listen carefully to the greeting, then contact the service provider and find out where the most recent outgoing calls were made from. Get the provider to check his messages and make a note of them. I also want you to contact Marisol Hinton's cell provider. I want a complete list of all of the incoming and outgoing calls made over the last ten days."

"I'm on it, Jesse," Perkins said.

Both officers hurried away.

Jesse looked at Bauer.

"Something I can do, Skipper?"

"Get a photo of Ryan Rooney. Easy enough to find on the Internet. I want you to show it to every motel and hotel in the area. See if any of them have laid eyes on him."

"Sure thing, Skipper."

Jesse opened his cell phone and called Molly.

"This is going to escalate," he said to her. "I want you to put a lid on it. No pronouncements. No publicity. Nada."

"Copy that."

"I want a full department meeting at six a.m. tomorrow."

"Got it."

After a moment, she said, "I'm sorry about Frankie."

"Any word from the hospital?"

"Nothing yet."

"Let me know?"

"The moment I hear anything," she said, and ended the call.

Jesse stared at the phone for a moment.

Crow walked over to him.

"What are you looking for," he said.

"Anything that might resemble a clue. Mostly relevant information regarding Ryan Rooney. Did he call her? If so, when? From where? Can his movements be traced to Paradise. That kind of stuff."

The two men were silent for a while.

"My watch," Crow said.

"Mine, too."

"Mostly mine."

"Don't beat yourself up. Whoever did it was ten steps ahead of us."

"It's got to be Rooney."

"We don't know that for certain."

"I want to go after him."

"Needle in a haystack."

"I still want to do it."

"Because?"

"Vengeance," Crow said.

44

The CSI unit arrived, followed by Captain Healy, the state Homicide commander.

"Another fine mess," Healy said.

"It is, isn't it," Jesse said.

They walked to Marisol's body, followed by the crime scene techs. They looked at her, small and bloodied. Then Jesse told Healy what he knew.

Peter Perkins approached them.

"No answer at either of his numbers," Perkins said, referring to his notepad. "His phone greeting says he's hiking in Grand Teton National Park and will be out of cell range for a number of days. Carrier says the greeting was recorded in Jackson Hole, Wyoming, one week ago. I also found a voice mail message from him on Marisol's cell. It, too, came from Jackson Hole. Also one week ago. There's been no activity on his phone since."

"Suggesting that he might actually be hiking in the Tetons," Healy said.

"Not likely," Jesse said.

"How so?"

"If he was driving across country, he could just as easily have taken the northern route, stopped in Wyoming, made the two calls, and then continued on his way here."

"Smoke and mirrors?"

"Be my guess," Jesse said.

"So where is he now?"

"That would be the question, wouldn't it?"

"Bauer wanted me to tell you that Rooney drives a late-model Toyota Prius," Perkins said. "He's put the description and the plate number on the wire."

"Thanks, Pete," Jesse said.

"No problem."

Perkins hurried away.

"Tell me again why you think it was the husband," Healy said. "He's some kind of movie star, right?"

"Not a star. An actor, though."

"Why do you think it's him?"

"Coply intuition."

"Gut rumbling, you mean."

"Eloquently stated."

"Thank you."

Jesse didn't say anything.

"There are going to be repercussions," Healy said.

"Meaning?"

"High-profile case like this, I'm betting that the first person I hear from will be Lucas Wellstein."

"The Boston FBI agent?"

"The very same. He'll want to get his fangs into this one."

"Can you stall him?"

"Hard to say. Once the tabloids blow this thing onto page one, he'll smell the ink and want some of it. I'll do my best to protect your jurisdiction. But I can't promise anything."

"He'll be a pain in the ass, right?"

"Worse."

Jesse entered Paradise General Hospital and checked in with the chief resident, Jim Lafferty, who told him that Frankie had pulled through the surgery and was now in recovery, where she would spend the rest of the night. Her prognosis was uncertain.

"She lost a great deal of blood," Lafferty said. "The bullet did some serious arterial and tissue damage. At the very least, we were able to repair the torn arteries and stabilize her. Now it's a question of hurry up and wait."

"What do you think," Jesse said.

"We'll know more in the morning."

"May I see her?"

"Not a good idea. She's unconscious and hooked up to a shit-load of IVs and monitoring devices."

Jesse sighed.

"She's in good hands, Jesse," Lafferty said. "She's resting comfortably. We're optimistic."

The two men shook hands.

Jesse looked at his watch and saw that it was nearly two a.m. He went home and sleeplessly waited for morning.

45

Jesse arrived at the station a little before six. He dropped his things on his desk, poured himself a mug of black coffee, and headed for the squad room.

The entire police force was there. Jesse took his seat at the head of the table.

"Good morning," he said. "Sorry to drag you in here so early. As you already know, this one's a bitch. One dead. One seriously wounded. Killer or killers still at large."

He looked at Suitcase.

"What's new from your end, Suit," he said.

"Movie's temporarily shut down. I spoke with Buddy Keller, the lead producer. He says they're waiting on a meeting between the studio production wonks and the insurance adjusters."

"When will he know?"

"Know what?"

"Whether or not the movie will resume production."

"He said probably today."

Jesse nodded.

He turned to Rich Bauer.

"Any luck with the photo?"

"A few people recognized Ryan Rooney," Bauer said. "But no one had seen him. I left copies of the picture at all of the motels and hotels."

"We need to expand the search so that it encompasses every rental unit in Paradise. Even those that aren't listed. If there's a room for rent, canvass it. I don't care where or what it is."

"I'm on it, Skipper."

"I also want you to hit every restaurant, bar, fast-food joint, supermarket, mini-mall, and big box store. By the time you're through, I want everyone in Paradise to be on the lookout for Mr. Ryan Rooney. Divvy it up. I want as many bodies on this as possible.

"Pete, I want you and Arthur to scour the Fisherman's Road neighborhood. A lot of the cottages are boarded up. Investigate them all. See if there have been any break-ins.

"We're looking for an armed and dangerous killer, people. If you should find this person, make every possible effort to apprehend him. But if that's not possible, if you're met with resistance of any kind, do everything in your power to protect yourself. Including shooting the son of a bitch, if it's necessary. Am I clear?"

Jesse looked around the table and made eye contact with his officers, all of whom nodded their assent.

"Captain Healy thinks we might be usurped by the FBI. Regardless of whether or not that happens, I want you to undertake as thorough an investigation as is humanly possible."

Jesse stood.

"Give Molly a list of who's in what vehicle. And I want each vehicle to check in with her every half hour. Good luck."

As the officers pushed back their chairs, Jesse motioned to Suitcase.

"Suit," he said. "Come see me when you have a moment. You, too, Dave."

He went back to his office.

He phoned Paradise General and got through to Dr. Lafferty.

"I've got nothing new to report, Jesse."

"No improvement?"

"No. She's still unconscious."

"Is that a good sign or a bad sign?"

"I wouldn't take it as any kind of sign. She experienced significant trauma. As I told you last night, she's stabilized, which is a good thing. But she's still not out of the woods. We're doing everything we can."

"You'll let me know if there's anything I can do?"

"I will."

"Thanks, Jim," Jesse said, and put down the phone.

He looked up and saw Molly standing in his doorway. " 'Anything,' " she said.

"No."

"Try not to obsess. It's gonna turn out okay. I know it."

"If you say so."

"I say so."

Suitcase stuck his head into Jesse's office.

"You wanted to see me," he said.

"I did."

"What's up?"

"Special assignment."

"For me?"

"Yes."

"What's the assignment?"

"I want you to make three arrests."

"Arrests?"

"Correct," Jesse said.

"You want me to arrest three people?"

"William J. Goodwin. Oscar LaBrea. Ida Fearnley."

"From the Department of Water and Power?"

"Exactly."

"On what charges?"

"Extortion. Grand theft. Threatening the life of a police officer."

"Wow," Suitcase said.

"Indeed," Jesse said.

"When do you want these arrests made?"

"This morning."

"Wow," Suitcase said.

"You'll need backup."

"Okay."

"Bring Steve Dickler and Bobby Harmon."

"Okay."

"Read them their rights and place them in separate cells in the tombs."

Suitcase didn't say anything.

"One more thing," Jesse said.

"What's that?"

"Oscar LaBrea may have suffered a recent facial accident. Take him down anyway. Cuffs and shackles. And add assault with a deadly weapon to his charges."

Both men were silent for a while.

"May I ask you a question, Jesse?"

"Shoot."

"What in the fuck happened?"

"Nothing good."

"What did they do?"

"Everything as charged."

"To you?"

"To me."

"Yikes."

"Exactly."

Suitcase stood up.

"Oscar LaBrea threatened you with a weapon?"

"He did."

"And you didn't kill him?"

"Astonishing, isn't it?"

"Is that why he suffered this so-called accident?"

"Possibly."

Suitcase stared at him for several moments.

"What did you do to him?"

"Let's just say his nose got out of joint."

Suitcase looked at him, then he turned and headed for the door.

"Suit," Jesse said.

Suitcase looked back at him.

"Let me know when it's done."

No sooner had Suitcase gone than Dave Muntz appeared.

"What's up," he said.

"Research," Jesse said.

"What kind of research?"

"I want you to scour the Internet. Check Facebook, Twitter, LinkedIn, Craigslist. Everything. I know it's a long shot, but anything's possible."

"You want me to look for information regarding Ryan Rooney?"

"I want you to hunt for the anomaly. Anything that seems

out of the ordinary. It's probably a wild-goose chase, but I don't think we should overlook anything."

Muntz nodded. He headed for the door. Then he turned back.

"I'm impressed," he said.

"Because I know about the Internet?"

"Yeah."

"I'm a barrelful of surprises," Jesse said. "You can't afford to ignore this stuff. Everyone seems to be tuned in. Maybe the killer was, too."

"Worth a try, I suppose."

"That's what I was thinking."

46

Jesse stopped off at the Town Hall on his way to the station.

He went to see Carter Hansen, who was alone in his office, staring at the ceiling.

"You heard," Jesse said.

"That poor girl," Hansen said.

"I'm sorry, Carter. I know how much this meant to you."

"To all of us."

Jesse didn't say anything.

"How's the other one? The Greenberg girl?"

"Stabilized."

"Will she pull through?"

"I hope so."

"Is it true that the husband is the prime suspect?"

"I'd have to believe so."

"Not the redskin?"

"The redskin? Jesus, Carter, what century are you living in?"

"He certainly had cause," Hansen said.

"Try not to bandy about your racism," Jesse said.

"Whatever," Hansen said. "I think he did it."

"You can't be serious," Jesse said.

"Dead serious," Hansen said. "Particularly given the way she spoke to him the other day."

"He didn't do it."

"How can you say that with such assurance?"

Jesse didn't say anything.

"I believe he did it," Hansen said. "I don't think that an actor could actually murder someone. Especially not his own wife."

"You're certainly entitled to your opinion, Carter, but you're wrong."

Jesse stood.

"I guess this wasn't such a good idea," he said.

"What's that supposed to mean?"

"I should have learned by now never to underestimate the depths of your buffoonery."

"The door's open," Hansen said.

"I noticed," Jesse said.

———

"You actually called him a buffoon," Molly said.

"In a manner of speaking," Jesse said.

They were sitting in Jesse's office. Jesse was drinking coffee.

"My tolerance factor is definitely diminished," Jesse said.

"And you're not afraid to let everyone know it."

"He's a moron."

"He's the head selectman."

"Which isn't a license to practice idiocy."

"It's a license to behave as he chooses."

"That's a load of crap."

Molly stood. She sighed.

"Pete Perkins called," she said.

"Can you get him for me, please?"

"Sore fingers, have we?"

"Don't start."

"I'll take it under advisement."

She left his office and after a few moments shouted, "Pete on line one."

"Thank you."

"You owe me."

Jesse picked up the call.

"What's up," he said.

"There was a break-in at one of the cottages near the movie location." Jesse didn't say anything. "Two doors away from the murder site. Kitchen window was smashed. Looks like someone entered the cottage through it and stayed for a while."

"Did you call in a CSI team?"

"We did. They just arrived."

"Let me know what they find."

"As soon as I know," Perkins said.

C aptain Healy on line four," Molly said.

"I was right," Healy said, when Jesse picked up.

"Meaning?"

"Lucas Wellstein."

"He phoned?"

"He not only phoned, he's on his way to Paradise."

"Should I go into hiding?"

"You might want to consider it. Oh, and I'm on my way also."

"Looking for ink, too?"

"Actually, I was hoping for a shot on *The View*."

Jesse didn't say anything. "You'll want to keep an eye on your temper," Healy said.

"Why would you say a thing like that?"

"You know why. I'll be there within the hour."

Healy ended the call. Jesse sat back in his chair.

He swiveled around and stared out the window.

———

Jesse noticed a black Crown Victoria sedan pull up in front of the station.

Four men climbed out. They wore identical black suits, gray ties, and dark sunglasses. They headed for the entrance.

After a few moments, Molly stuck her head into Jesse's office.

"Special Agent Lucas Wellstein of the Federal Bureau of Investigation to see you."

"Tell him I'm not in."

"Too late."

"You mean you told him I was here?"

"Proudly."

"Jesus."

Lucas Wellstein pushed past Molly and entered the office. He approached Jesse with his hand extended.

"Lucas Wellstein," he said.

Jesse stood and accepted Wellstein's hand.

"It's nice to meet you, Chief Stone," Wellstein said.

"Jesse."

"Excuse me?"

"The name's Jesse."

"Okay. Jesse," Wellstein said, peering at him more closely.

Wellstein was an old-looking young man with an eminently forgettable moon-shaped face that featured coal-black eyes, which radiated paranoia and suspicion. His furtive glances from behind his horn-rimmed glasses, coupled with his self-conscious awkwardness, put Jesse in mind of Richard Nixon.

"We're here regarding the Hinton murder case," Wellstein said.

"And so fast, too."

"Can you take us to the crime scene?"

"I can."

Jesse didn't move.

"Now," Wellstein said.

"You mean you want to go now?"

"Yes."

Jesse stood and looked at the door.

"Would you like me to take you there," he said.

"Yes. I would."

"Then please feel free to follow."

Jesse looked at Molly, whose full-faced grin forced him to turn away.

Then it was on to the crime scene.

47

Captain Healy was already at the scene when Jesse and the cavalry arrived.

Lucas Wellstein approached him.

"Captain," he said to Healy.

"Lucas," Healy said.

"Where is everybody," Wellstein said.

"Meaning," Jesse said.

"The movie people. Where are they?"

"Once they got word that production had been suspended, they packed up and left."

"Left town?"

"Probably they just went back to their local accommodations."

"I'm sorry to hear that."

"Sorry to hear what," Jesse said.

"I had hoped they would remain on the site. So that I might question them."

"We had no idea you would be coming. We did speak with each member of the cast and crew, and collected contact information for all of them."

" 'We'?"

"My officers and I."

Wellstein smiled sardonically.

"I'm sure you did an excellent job," he said. "I still wish they had stayed. But, hey, that's water under the bridge now, isn't it?"

His smile reeked of both personal and professional insincerity.

Jesse didn't say anything.

"We'll be taking over from here," Wellstein said. "Thank you for all that you've done."

"Would you like to see the information we compiled?"

"Not just yet. I'll get back to you about it."

Neither Jesse nor Healy said anything.

"Can you show me the crime scene?"

Jesse led him to the spot where Marisol and Frankie had been shot.

"Killing took place right here," Jesse said. "CSI unit already did their inspection."

"That's damned fine police work, Stone," Wellstein said.

"You should also commend Captain Healy for that. I'm sure he'll be appreciative."

Wellstein looked at Jesse.

"Are you being condescending, Chief Stone?"

"Jesse."

"I don't take kindly to attitude . . . Jesse."

"Neither do I."

The two men stared at each other.

"Do we have a problem," Wellstein said.

"I would hope not," Jesse said.

"I would hope not, as well."

Jesse didn't say anything.

"I think I can handle things from here," Wellstein said.

"I would hope so," Jesse said.

t's uncanny," Healy said as he and Jesse wandered away.

"What is," Jesse said.

"How you manage to piss people off."

"It's a gift."

"Lucas Wellstein isn't someone you want to be on the wrong side of."

"Too late now."

"Can I ask you a question?"

Jesse didn't say anything.

"What exactly was it that set you off?"

"I beg your pardon," Jesse said.

"What about him got your goat?"

"Pretty much everything."

"What everything?"

"Quit hocking me. You know exactly what I mean."

Healy smiled.

"He is a bit of a shit," Healy said.

"And that's just for openers," Jesse said.

48

Jesse had arranged to meet Frankie's father, Henry Greenberg, at the hospital. He was already there when Jesse arrived.

Greenberg was a handsome man who was aging well. Jesse guessed him to be in his late fifties, still fit and youthful in appearance.

"Jesse Stone," Jesse said as he approached Mr. Greenberg.

"Hank Greenberg."

"Like the baseball player?"

"Better him than that crook from AIG."

"Nice to meet you, Mr. Greenberg."

"Hank."

"Hank."

"I've spoken with Dr. Lafferty," Greenberg said. "He seems optimistic."

"That's the feeling I get."

"Can you tell me what exactly happened?"

Jesse explained that it was primarily a case of being in the wrong place at the wrong time. That she hadn't been targeted.

"I'm sure she'd be happy to know that you're here," Jesse said.

"Lafferty said they would be moving her into a private room so that I can sit with her."

"That's a good sign."

"I hope so. She's all I've got."

Jesse gave Greenberg his card and wrote his cell-phone number on it. He promised to stop by again.

"This is very nice of you," Greenberg said.

"I'm rooting for her," Jesse said.

D id you really think you'd get away with it," Jesse said.

He was seated on a straight-backed chair in the center aisle of the tombs, between the two rows of three cells each, in front of the one occupied by William J. Goodwin.

"Get away with what," Goodwin said.

"Well," Jesse said, "the crime, for starters."

"We never thought anyone would catch on," Goodwin said.

"You thought the rate hikes would continue to go unnoticed," Jesse said.

"Yes," Goodwin said.

Ida Fearnley was in the cell across from Goodwin's, sitting on the cot, her head bowed.

Oscar LaBrea sat on a stool in the cell adjacent to Goodwin's. His nose was heavily bandaged. The skin around his eyes was a deeply bruised blue-black, giving him the look of a demented badger.

The three of them presented a sad tableau.

"It's not that your ideas don't have merit," Jesse said. "You make a compelling argument, and I'd like to believe that if you had gone about doing things legally, you might have been able to get some changes made."

Goodwin didn't say anything.

"Abusing the law never serves anyone's purposes. How could you not have known that?"

Goodwin looked at the floor.

"What will happen to us," Ida said.

"That's for the courts to decide. I'll be presenting your case to the district attorney this afternoon. He'll take it from there."

None of them spoke.

Jesse stood.

"For what it's worth, you have my sympathies. You served the people of this town honorably for many years."

Jesse stepped over to LaBrea's cell. He stared in at him. LaBrea shied away.

"Do you really think you could have done it," Jesse said.

LaBrea didn't say anything. He was breathing through his mouth.

"You don't have the cojones," Jesse said.

LaBrea remained silent.

Jesse turned away from him in disgust.

There was nothing left to say.

It was dusk when Jesse opened the door to his house and was greeted by a complaining Mildred Memory. She hadn't appreciated his absence and let him know it. She followed him into the kitchen, where he put his service belt and pistol on the counter and then fed her.

He poured himself a scotch.

When Mildred had finished eating, Jesse picked her up and sat down in one of the armchairs in the living room.

As a show of gratitude, she proceeded to lick his hand with her sandpaper tongue, then stretched out across his lap and rested her head on his forearm, pinning him to the chair. She purred contentedly.

Jesse sat back and thought about Frankie Greenberg and of the feelings he had developed for her, which he had not yet taken the time to analyze. She had suddenly appeared in his life, and they found themselves together. He liked her. He enjoyed spending time with her.

But he understood how new they were, and how uncertain. And how unlikely it would be for their relationship to continue once the movie was over.

What did that say to him? That he was attracted to dead-end relationships? That commitment continued to elude him by his own choice?

He thought briefly about Jenn and wondered where she was and who she was with. He had successfully rid himself of the burden of his ex-wife, yet at times like this, unsettled times, she still entered his mind.

He considered calling her, but he knew better than to invite her back into his life.

Here he was, once again adrift, his premises uncertain.

He reached around Mildred and poured himself another scotch. But he stopped himself from drinking it. He realized he was on the brink. He put the glass down.

He couldn't bring himself to dislodge the sleeping cat from his lap, so he leaned back in his chair and struggled to make himself more comfortable.

Then he was asleep.

Ryan Rooney couldn't sleep.

Finally he got out of bed and went to the darkened living room. He replayed the shootings over and over in his mind. He was happy to have administered a proper fate to Marisol. He cherished the look in her eye when she realized that it was him. She got what she deserved.

As for Frankie Greenberg, he was both astonished that he had shot her and remorseful for the deed.

It was a knee-jerk reaction, he kept telling himself. He hadn't intended to do it. When she started toward him, he shot her in self-defense.

Maybe it was the crystal meth. Perhaps his judgment had been impaired.

To his great surprise, he was consumed by guilt. He couldn't get it out of his mind.

He would now be forced to change his plans. He had rented the cabin for a month. He would stay there and wait it out. He would make his move when more time had elapsed and surveillance became lax.

He would stay off the highways. He would take the back roads. He would head north to Maine, where he could illegally cross the border into Quebec and disappear into the Canadian wilderness.

He reached for his paraphernalia and his Shabu rock.

He breathed the air of invincibility.

I'll get through this, he thought.

49

Molly arrived at the station to find Courtney waiting outside.

The two women didn't speak. They eyed each other warily as Molly unlocked the door and they went inside.

"Would 'Good morning' be too much for you," Molly said.

"Being here wasn't my idea."

"That's not what I asked."

"You could've just as easily said it yourself."

"It's generally good manners for younger people to offer greetings to their elders."

"Blah, blah, blah," Courtney said.

"Charming," Molly said.

Molly showed her the supply closet. The cleaning equipment was inside. She picked up a mop and showed it to Courtney.

"This is a mop," she said.

Courtney didn't say anything.

"You ever see one before?"

Courtney snorted.

"I'll bet you never handled one before," Molly said.

"Is this what it's gonna be like being here?"

"Get used to it."

Molly withdrew a handful of ancient rags and a can of Endust.

"You know how to use this stuff?"

"No. Show me."

"Figure it out for yourself. Go dust the bookcases and the desktops, and everything else that looks like it might have dust on it. When you're finished with that, go downstairs and mop the floors. And when that's done, clean the toilets."

"The toilets?"

"That's right."

"What if I refuse?"

"Then you'll find yourself standing in front of Judge Weissberg again with the female house of detention looming large in your future."

"This isn't fair."

"You should've thought of that before you broke the law."

Courtney picked up a mop, the Endust, and the rags. She headed for the squad room.

"Hey," Molly said.

Courtney turned back.

"Try to enjoy yourself," Molly said.

"Whatever," Courtney said.

They had agreed to meet for breakfast at Daisy's at seven. Jesse arrived promptly, but when he got to the table, he found Lucas Wellstein already in full rant. His audience was Captain Healy.

Beside him was a stack of newspapers, each emblazoned with a Marisol Hinton headline.

"You're late," he said to Jesse, then continued unabated. "We checked out the break-in at the cottage. It's likely that the killer was staying there. We found food remnants and drug-related debris. We're running tests now."

"Are you thinking it was Ryan Rooney," Jesse said.

"It's possible. But who's to say he's not deep in the bowels of the Grand Tetons, eating pork and beans from a can, and that someone else did it."

"I am," Jesse said.

"I'm sorry," Wellstein said.

"I'm to say," Jesse said.

"To say what?"

"That he's not deep in the bowels of the Grand Tetons, eating pork and beans from a can."

"Then where is he?"

"I don't know."

"But you can say with a degree of certainty that he's not in the Grand Tetons."

"Yes."

"Either back it up with facts, Stone, or keep your opinion to yourself."

"Are you eliminating him from suspicion?"

"Ryan Rooney?"

"Yes."

"No. But I also like someone else."

"Who?"

"Wilson Cromartie."

Jesse didn't say anything.

"His DNA is everywhere."

"And that's why you suspect him?"

"That's part of the reason."

"And the other part?"

"She appears to have been verbally abusing him publicly."

"He didn't do it."

"I believe the evidence is inconclusive. It was nighttime. Hinton and Greenberg were sitting apart from the action. In the dark. Who's to say your Mr. Cromartie didn't step up to them and fire?"

"He had no cause."

"He had plenty of cause. If she was disrespectful of him in public, who knows how she behaved in private. What if she resisted his romantic advances."

" 'His romantic advances'?"

"He was sharing a hotel suite with a beautiful woman. Who's to know what took place between them?"

"Nothing took place between them. And they weren't sharing the suite. He was in an adjoining room."

"Thank you for your opinion, Stone."

"Since when did I become Stone?"

Wellstein didn't say anything.

"Yesterday it was Chief Stone. Then it was Jesse. Today it's Stone. How did I fall from grace so quickly?"

"Don't get into my face with your bullshit," Wellstein said.

"My bullshit?"

"That's right."

"Let me guess," Jesse said after a moment. "Princeton."

"I beg your pardon?"

"I'm guessing Princeton. With your extraordinary people skills and your incredible charm, you had to have graduated from Princeton."

"Fuck off," Wellstein said.

"See, I knew it."

"Where's your bodyguard now?"

"My bodyguard?"

"You're the one who hired him."

"Marisol Hinton hired him," Jesse said.

"On your recommendation. Where is he?"

"Last time I saw him was yesterday."

"Well, today he's disappeared."

"Ryan Rooney did it," Jesse said.

"Why don't we wait until all the facts are in before arriving at that conclusion," Wellstein said.

Jesse stood.

"You know where to find me if you need me," he said to Lucas Wellstein.

He glanced briefly at Captain Healy, then left the restaurant.

Jesse was heading for his office, and as he passed Molly's desk, he motioned for her to follow.

She sighed, stood, and joined him.

"I hate to admit it, but you were right," she said as she sat down in the chair opposite his desk.

Jesse looked at her.

"Girl's a first-class pain in the ass."

"It's our job to change that. To show her the light."

"I need to fish out a copy of my contract."

Jesse didn't say anything.

"Showing the light to some candy-assed debutante isn't in my job description."

"But think how gratified you'll be when the job's done."

"In the immortal words of the debutante herself, 'Blah, blah, blah.'"

Jesse didn't say anything.

"When she finishes dusting, I'm gonna have her mop up downstairs," Molly said.

"Excellent. Don't let her forget the toilets."

"Oh, don't worry yourself about that."

The phone rang, and Molly reached across Jesse's desk to answer it.

"Suitcase," she said.

She handed him the phone and walked out of his office.

"What's up," Jesse said.

"*A Taste of Arsenic* has been officially canceled."

Jesse didn't say anything.

"Movie's in the process of shutting down," Suitcase said. "Vehicles and personnel are disappearing fast."

"Hansen know?"

"He's watching it happen."

"Keep in touch."

"I will." Jesse hung up the phone. He sat back in his chair and thought for a while.

Just like that, the movie was over. The FBI had arrived, and the investigation into Marisol's death now belonged to them. There was still no sign of Ryan Rooney. Captain Healy mentioned that FBI agents were on their way to Grand Teton National Park to search for him there. Crow had gone to ground. Amazing how quickly things changed.

After a while, Jesse left the office and headed for Boston.

50

Jesse wandered through the chrome-and-glass lobby of the Cone, Oakes, and Baldwin building on Constitution Square and boarded the high-speed elevator for the ride to the penthouse. Once there, he asked a receptionist to inform Rita Fiore that he had arrived for their appointment.

There was something electric about Rita when she strode through the big glass doors. Her deep green Donna Karan suit set off her fiery red hair. The knee-length skirt had just the right flare at the hemline to showcase her remarkable legs. The smile on her face reflected both curiosity and her own appreciation of Jesse's appeal.

"Jesse Stone," she said, with the faintest hint of amusement in her voice.

"None other," he said.

She guided him back through the glass doors that led to her office. Her assistant asked if he needed anything. "Coffee would be nice," Jesse said.

"Me, too," Rita said.

He sat in front of her desk.

"What brings Jesse Stone into my parlor," she said.

"You mean other than the opportunity to appreciate your legs?"

"Occasionally there are other reasons."

"I'm riding the horns of a dilemma."

"How poetic."

He told her the William J. Goodwin story.

"The combination of his physical size, his voice, and the way he dresses makes him so stereotypically laughable that he's often underrated and an easy target for ridicule. Especially in the corridors where the big boys roam. What he did was wrong. Unquestionably so. What's eating at me, though, is the belief that he himself was wronged. He paid an inordinately hefty price for his physical misfortunes."

"It wouldn't be the first time such a thing has happened."

"I understand too well how cruel the real world can be. What I don't know is whether his actions are defensible under the law."

"Which is why you're here."

"That and the legs, of course."

"Of course," Rita said.

They sat silently for a while.

"Here's this weird-looking little guy who hits upon a potentially viable solution to a burgeoning problem and seeks to have it considered seriously at the highest levels. He's articulate. He's passionate. But he is who he is, and no one will take him seriously. He cracks. He takes matters into his own hands."

"You want to know whether a crime is punishable if it was provoked by damaging and prejudicial behavior."

Jesse didn't say anything.

She struggled to find the exact definition that suited her.

"If the accused was the victim of persecution," Rita said, "and, as a result, suffered diminished faculties and distorted judgment, and then subsequently committed a crime that he believed he had been goaded into committing, is that crime punishable under the law?"

"That would be the question," Jesse said.

She thought about it for a while.

"I'd need to talk it over with my partners," she said.

"Meaning?"

"It might make for a compelling argument. Would a jury see fit to convict in the face of it? I'd need to consider that some more."

Jesse didn't say anything.

"This is important to you," she said.

"Apparently, although for the life of me, I can't figure out why."

"Strange how a thing grabs you."

"I'd like for him to find some measure of redemption," Jesse said. "A feeling that in the end, he had made a difference."

"Even in the face of LaBrea and the gun?"

"Yes."

"You're an odd duck, Jesse Stone."

He smiled.

They stood.

"Thanks for your consideration, Rita."

They shook hands.

"It was nice to see you," she said.

"Ditto."

51

On his way back from Boston, Jesse stopped in at Paradise General Hospital. He found Frankie Greenberg's new room. Her father, Hank, was seated next to her bed. She was still unconscious.

At Jesse's suggestion, Hank joined him in the hallway.

"Any progress?"

"Dr. Lafferty said she appeared to be inching toward consciousness. He noticed some rapid eye movement, and when he was questioning her, her facial expressions kept changing. He was encouraged."

"What's next?"

"Continued progress, hopefully."

"Do you need anything?"

"Thanks, no. They're taking very good care of me here."

"You'll call me if there's any change?"

"I will."

The two men said their good-byes, and Jesse headed home.

Jesse found Healy's car parked in front of the footbridge.

He crossed the bridge and walked around the house to the porch, where he found the captain dozing on the sofa, Mildred Memory asleep on his lap.

Healy's eyes fluttered open when Jesse arrived.

"I thought I'd stop by on my way home," he said. "See how you're doin'."

Jesse unlocked the porch doors and opened them.

"So how you doin'?"

"Scotch?"

"On the rocks."

Jesse went inside and fixed two drinks. Healy stayed put, not wishing to disturb the cat.

Jesse returned, handed Healy his scotch, then sat down and took a sip of his own.

"The times, they are a-changin'," Jesse said.

"Woody Guthrie?"

"Bob Dylan."

"After my time," Healy said.

"Most things are."

"Your favorite person was asking about you."

"And that would be?"

"Lucas Wellstein, of course. He thinks you might know the whereabouts of a certain Native American gentleman."

"He's still a person of interest?"

"To Lucas he is, yes."

"He's wrong."

"Maybe, but he still thinks you may be withholding information."

Jesse didn't say anything.

"All that's preventing him from pouncing on you is the fact that Ryan Rooney has disappeared also."

"Maybe they're together," Jesse said.

"Try not to be cute, okay."

"It's hard for me not to be cute."

"Do you know where he is?"

"Crow?"

"Yes."

"No."

"Have you tried to find him?"

"No."

"Would you? In the interests of cooperation with a federal agency."

"I'll take it under advisement."

"You're one incredible ballbuster."

"Everyone says that."

"And it's no wonder."

Healy took a sip of his scotch and stood, dislodging Mildred.

"You could at least try to take this a bit more seriously," he said.

"Crow didn't do it."

Healy didn't say anything.

"Ryan Rooney killed her."

"I'm not doubting you."

"Then what's your point?"

"I'm a big fan of peace in the valley," Healy said.

"Woody Guthrie?"

Healy stared at him.

"Maybe if you hummed a few bars," Jesse said.

"I knew this was a mistake."

"The scotch was good, though."

"The scotch was excellent," Healy said.

He took one last pull on his glass, looked around for a few moments, then stepped off the porch and headed for his car.

52

Jesse was at the station early the next morning. He flipped on the lights in his office, then poured himself a coffee.

Despite Molly's critical glare, he grabbed a jelly donut and headed past her desk and back toward his office.

She followed him.

"Do you ever think about the consequences of filling your face with globs of saturated fat and cholesterol," she said.

"Some day they'll discover that donuts are actually good for you."

He took a bite and chewed it slowly enough to gain her attention.

"Swallow it, will you. You're making me nauseous."

"You're the one wandered in here uninvited. It's my office, and I'll eat what I choose in it."

"Why are you doing it?"

"Doing what?"

"Wasting your time with that awful child."

"You mean Courtney?"

"Yes."

"I think she's gotten a bum steer."

Molly didn't say anything.

"Her parents," he said.

"What about them?"

"They're the cause."

"So you see her as a victim."

"I do."

"Which appeals to your hyperactive sense of responsibility?"

"I think I can help her."

"Point made."

"Maybe you're right. Maybe she's incorrigible. But just maybe she's not."

Molly didn't say anything.

"She deserves a chance."

"A chance at what?"

"At seeing the other side of the coin."

"Which you're planning to show her."

"Yes."

"And if you're wrong?"

"At least I'll have tried."

Molly stared at him.

"Was there something else that you wanted," he said.

She handed him the messages.

He thumbed through them.

"Dave Muntz called," he said.

"That's what the message says."

Jesse looked at her and then dialed the number.

"This is David," Muntz said.

"What's up?"

"Craigslist."

"What about it?"

"I called Craigslist."

"And?"

"I asked about all of their real estate listings for this area during the last few months. Turns out that a Boston resident who owns a cabin in South Hamilton had it up for rent."

"Okay."

"It caught my attention because it was so close to Paradise, and because it was the only listing for the area. So I figured what the hell, and called the owner."

"Okay."

"He told me that he rented the cabin for a month."

"Okay."

"It's rented."

"Can you help me out a bit more, Dave. What in the fuck are you talking about?"

"According to the owner, the entire transaction was carried out on Craigslist."

"So?"

"The renter listed his address as Beverly Hills, California. His check was drawn on a Beverly Hills bank. He picked up the keys from a prearranged post office box in Salem."

Jesse didn't say anything.

"The renter lists his name as Buddy Fairbanks."

"Who's Buddy Fairbanks?"

"Are you ready for this, Jesse?"

"Come on, Dave."

"Buddy Fairbanks is the name of the character that Ryan Rooney played in *Tomorrow We Love*."

"How do you know?"

"I looked it up."

"Where's the cabin?"

Muntz provided Jesse with the information.

"I'll check it out," Jesse said.

"I thought you might."

"This is very good police work, Dave."

"Thanks, Jesse."

He hung up the phone and stared at Molly.

"Good news?"

"Maybe."

"What are you gonna do?"

"Pay a visit to South Hamilton."

"You're not going to inform Agent Wellstein?"

"Not yet."

"Why not?"

"Because I don't like him."

Molly shrugged.

"Never let it be said that maturity clouded your judgment," she said.

She returned to her desk.

Jesse picked up the phone and dialed.

"What," said the voice on the other end of the line.

"Bingo," Jesse said.

53

Jesse dropped Crow off at a clearing in the woods, a mile or so from Ryan Rooney's rented cabin.

Crow had never left Paradise. Since moving out of Marisol's hotel, he had been living in a makeshift lean-to that he had carved into the sand dunes at North Beach. The cool fall weather ensured his privacy, and he had always been more comfortable living amidst nature than among people.

Jesse watched as Crow unloaded a few things from the trunk of his car. The only weapon he carried was his bowie knife.

"That's it? A knife," Jesse said.

Crow nodded.

"This guy is armed."

"I'll take my chances."

"Cell phone?"

"Shirt pocket."

"You'll call me," Jesse said.

Crow nodded.

"How do you say 'Good luck' in Apache," Jesse said.

"Go get 'em, kemosabe."

"I knew I shouldn't have asked."

The two men looked at each other.

"This means a lot to me, Jesse," Crow said.

"Then try not to fuck it up," Jesse said.

Crow smiled, then trotted off into the woods.

Ryan Rooney heard the sound of an approaching vehicle. The cabin was hidden deep enough in the woods that it was impossible to hear the highway traffic. Someone was definitely headed his way.

He peeked through the curtains at the front window. A police cruiser was inching its way toward the cabin.

As a preventive measure, Ryan had packed a duffel bag in case he had to make a quick getaway.

He grabbed the duffel, opened the kitchen door, and fled into the woods.

———

Jesse got out of the cruiser and approached the cabin. His Colt Commander automatic pistol was in his hand.

He knocked on the door.

There was no response.

"Police," he said. "Please exit the premises with your hands in the air."

Nothing happened.

He turned the doorknob. It was locked.

He walked the perimeter of the cabin. When he reached the back door, he tried the handle. It was unlocked. He went inside.

He carefully checked each room. The cabin was empty. He holstered his Colt and looked around, careful not to disturb anything, so that he wouldn't leave a trail that might capture the attention of a CSI team.

The occupant was gone. He had left in a hurry.

The bed was unmade. There were unwashed dishes in the sink and uneaten food on the counter. A recently washed pair of Jockey shorts hung over the shower curtain rod.

Satisfied, he left the cabin by way of the kitchen. He wiped the doorknob of prints. He did the same with the front door. He returned to his cruiser.

He leaned back in his seat and settled himself for the wait.

He had brought a Thermos of coffee and a couple of sandwiches from Daisy's. He lowered the cruiser's windows, allowing the cool fall air in. He listened to the sounds of the forest and he breathed deeply.

Despite himself, he dozed off, awakening with a start by the intrusion of a strange noise.

Two squirrels were sitting on the hood of the cruiser, absorbing the warmth of the slow-cooling engine. They stared at him through the windshield.

He stared back.

Evidently they didn't perceive him to be a threat.

The three of them stayed that way for a while.

The sound of Jesse's cell phone alarmed the squirrels. They leapt from the hood of the cruiser and disappeared into the woods.

"It's done," Crow said.

"How will I find him?"

"The screaming should begin shortly."

"The screaming?"

"Yes."

"Where are you?"

"Just outside New Haven."

"New Haven, Connecticut?"

"Yes."

"That's more than an hour from here."

"It is."

"How could you be in New Haven?"

"It took me five minutes to find him, ten more to prepare him, and then I left."

"Prepare him," Jesse said.

"Yes."

Jesse didn't say anything.

"Thanks to the miracle of modern chemistry, he's sleeping like a baby right now, but he'll be waking up real soon and real fast."

"And you can't tell me where he is?"

"I promise you'll know within minutes."

Jesse didn't say anything.

"Wanishi," Crow said.

"Which means?"

"Good wishes to you, my friend," Crow said, and ended the call.

Jesse stared out at the woods through the windshield.

Then the screaming began.

The screams led Jesse to a small clearing. Ryan Rooney was lying spread-eagle on the ground, his hands and feet tied to four posts that were firmly hammered into the hardened earth. He was screaming at the top of his lungs.

He was naked, and his body had been smeared with what appeared to be honey. Red ants swarmed all over him, and angry welts were already visible beneath the honey glaze.

When Rooney spotted Jesse, he screamed, "Help me."

Jesse knelt down beside him.

"Ryan Rooney," he said.

"Get them off of me," Ryan screamed.

"You're Ryan Rooney?"

"Yes. Yes, for crissakes. I'm Ryan Rooney."

"I'm charging you with the murder of Marisol Hinton."

Rooney screamed louder.

"Get me out of this."

Jesse looked at him for several moments. Then he grabbed his cell phone and punched in a number.

"Paradise police," Molly said.

"I've got him. Call out the reserves."

After telling her how to find him, he hung up.

Jesse released Rooney from his bindings and got him on his feet. Rooney tried to brush the ants away, but they clung to his skin, bound by the honey. He was still screaming when Jesse read him his rights.

A squad car and an ambulance pulled into the clearing.

The two EMTs used an antiseptic spray on Rooney, who continued his grotesque dance until the last of the ants either dropped off or died.

Then he fell to the ground and began to sob.

Suitcase Simpson, who had been in the lead car with Arthur Angstrom, stood beside Jesse, taking it all in.

"Ryan Rooney?"

"That would be he," Jesse said.

"Will I be taking him into custody?"

"You will."

"Should I read him his rights?"

"I already did."

"While he was screaming?"

"Between screams."

"How do you suppose this happened," Suitcase said.

"I wouldn't know."

Suitcase looked at him.

"Crow?"

"Beats me."

"You're not telling me, right?"

"How could you think such a thing," Jesse said.

Only after Rooney had been sedated, strapped onto a gurney, and lifted into the ambulance did Jesse punch a number into his phone.

Captain Healy answered.

"You can tell your friend that a certain person of interest will arrive at Paradise General in about ten minutes," Jesse said.

"Say that again."

"We found Ryan Rooney. He's on his way to the hospital."

"Was he wounded?"

"In a manner of speaking."

"What's that supposed to mean?"

"He was the victim of a vicious ant attack."

"Ants?"

"Red ones. Lots of them."

"In Massachusetts?"

"Yes."

"No."

"Infestations of red ants have been part of the ecological systems not only of Massachusetts, but of most of New England and southeast Canada since the early 1900s."

"I don't believe it."

"You could look it up."

Healy was quiet for a few moments. "Crow, right?"

"Beats me."

"Red ants?"

"Nasty ones," Jesse said.

"Had to have been Crow."

"I wouldn't know."

Healy sighed. "I'll inform Wellstein," he said.

"Excellent idea," Jesse said.

54

t was all over the evening news. Special Agent Lucas Wellstein stood before the microphones in front of Paradise General Hospital, fielding questions from reporters and newscasters.

He credited the FBI with the arrest and thanked Captain Healy for his assistance. He made no mention of Jesse.

The case took off when cell-phone photos and videos began to appear on TMZ and other websites, showing Ryan Rooney being carried from the ambulance.

Close-up shots revealed a face rendered all but unrecognizable by vivid red welts. He seemed incoherent and appeared to be sobbing.

The coverage went viral, raising questions as to exactly what had happened to him. The press and the public couldn't get enough of the story. Soon the tabloids were screaming cover-up.

Jesse watched it all on the TV in Frankie Greenberg's room, enjoying himself immensely. Hank Greenberg watched with him.

Frankie remained unconscious.

When the footage of Ryan arriving at the hospital appeared once again, Jesse smiled.

When he looked over at her, he saw that Frankie's eyes were open.

"Hey," he said.

"Hey yourself," she said hoarsely.

She looked around.

"Daddy?"

Hank hurried to her bedside. He held her in his arms. He was unable to control his tears.

"Welcome back, honey," he said.

55

J esse pushed past the media barrage outside of the station. Lucas Wellstein was waiting for him in his office.

"I'm getting slammed," Lucas said.

Jesse didn't say anything.

"There's a media backlash stemming from those damned cell-phone pictures. Everyone's clamoring for information about why Rooney looked the way he did."

Jesse remained silent.

"Just what went down out there," Wellstein said.

"You mean what happened to him?"

"Yes."

"Looks like he passed out and fell on top of an anthill."

"Don't fuck with me, Stone."

"Why, whatever do you mean?"

"You know what I think," Wellstein said.

Jesse didn't say anything.

"I think you and that damned Indian set him up."

"Why would you think that?"

"When did you learn he was out there?"

"I received an anonymous phone call saying that someone was in the woods, screaming his head off. I investigated and found Mr. Rooney. I called for backup, then phoned Captain Healy and asked him to inform you."

"Bullshit," Wellstein said.

Jesse didn't say anything.

"I could have your balls for this."

"I don't think so."

"What makes you so sure of yourself?"

"Your job is to quell the media furor. Exacerbating it would be a bad idea."

"So you set me up, too."

"I'm just a small-town cop. Mostly I write parking tickets."

"You're so full of shit, Stone."

"Was there anything else?"

"No."

Jesse stood.

"I'll refrain from voicing my entire opinion, Agent Wellstein, but suffice it to say, I think you're a disgrace to your service."

"Like I give a rat's ass what you think."

"A wise man once told me that people generally behave in the same manner toward everyone. You might want to consider the trails that you're blazing, Wellstein. You meet the same people on the way down as you met on the way up, if you get my drift."

Jesse walked over and opened the door.

"Happy trails, pardner," he said.

R ita Fiore on line two," Molly said.

Jesse picked up the call.

"Rita?"

"We'll take it," she said.

Jesse didn't say anything.

"We want to interview Goodwin as soon as we can. Once that's done, we'll file a motion to set bail. If it's okay with you, my associate and I would like to head up to Paradise now."

"Okay."

Rita didn't say anything.

After a moment, Jesse said, "Why?"

"Why did we take the case?"

"Yes."

"Obviously we'll know more once we've had a look at the paperwork and conducted some interviews, but let's just say that we're intrigued. We also have interest in the climate issue. We appreciate Mr. Goodwin's concerns about the worldwide water crisis. Regardless of the outcome, Cone, Oakes looks at this case as a means of further advancing the cause for reconsideration of this issue. We expect that the case will generate a fair amount of media attention."

"Which is why you decided to take it?"

"Partly. Yes."

"You lawyers are a strange lot."

"Tell me about it," she said.

The firm of Cone, Oakes, and Baldwin has agreed to handle your case," Jesse said to William J. Goodwin.

"Why would they do that," Goodwin said.

"You'll have to ask them yourself. Rita Fiore is on her way here now."

"Will she get us out of jail," Ida Fearnley said.

"After she has a better handle on each of your stories, I believe she'll seek bail."

"What do you mean," Goodwin said.

"I'm a cop, not a lawyer. But it's my understanding that after she interviews each of you, she'll petition the court on your behalf."

"To get us out of here," Ida said.

"Yes."

They were all silent for a while.

"I've heard of this Rita Fiore," Goodwin said. "She's supposedly quite good."

"You need someone quite good," Jesse said.

"So I realize," Goodwin said.

56

t's Rita," Molly said.

Jesse picked up the call.

"They made bail," Rita said.

"So they'll be getting out?"

"As soon as possible. Can I ask a dumb question?"

"Will it be a hard dumb question?"

"He's strange, isn't he?"

"Why would you say that?"

"He was surprisingly evasive. I told him we'd need access to his financial records. Also we'd need to interview the officials at state who refused to speak with him."

"And?"

"Maybe it's just me, but he seemed peeved."

Jesse didn't say anything.

"It's probably just me. In any event, they're getting out. He ponied up bail for the three of them. I've made an appointment with him for tomorrow. In the meantime, I've got my associate and my investigator swarming all over it. We'll see what they uncover."

Jesse didn't say anything.

"I've got goose bumps, Jesse," Rita said.

"Goose bumps?"

"Yes."

"Why?"

"I'm hoping it's not because someone's walking on my grave," she said.

You ever been to Daisy's," Jesse said.

He pulled his cruiser into traffic and headed west. Courtney was sitting beside him.

"What's Daisy's?"

"Only the finest diner in all the land."

"Yeah, right," Courtney said.

"You'll see."

They were silent until Jesse pulled into Daisy's lot and parked.

"Voilà," he said.

"Why are you doing this?"

"Because it's time for lunch."

"What if I don't want lunch?"

"You don't really have a choice."

She looked at Jesse.

He got out of the cruiser. After a moment, Courtney got out as well. They went inside.

Daisy showed them to a booth and offered them menus, but Jesse waved her off.

"Two turkey burgers with cheese, sweet-potato fries, and at least one vanilla shake. Courtney, this is Daisy. Daisy, Courtney."

"Hi, Courtney," Daisy said.

"Hi."

"You gonna join the big guy and accessorize your burger with one of my famous shakes, guaranteed to clog your arteries and do serious damage to your heart?"

Courtney smiled.

"Does it come in chocolate?"

"Does the Pope wear a cassock," Daisy said.

"Chocolate."

Daisy smiled at them.

"Two health-food specials," she called out to the chef.

Then she walked away.

Courtney looked around.

"This is okay," she said.

"Surprising you haven't been here before."

"My parents would never come to a place like this."

"Why not?"

"You're kidding, right?"

She scanned the crowded restaurant.

"Is Daisy a friend of yours?"

"She is. I was the first one in line on the day she opened."

"Really?"

"Yep. She's been clogging my arteries for nearly five years now."

"I still don't know why you're taking me to lunch," she said.

"Everybody's gotta eat lunch. Particularly if they're performing physical labor."

Daisy returned with the burgers and shakes.

"If need be," she said, "I can have EMTs here within minutes."

"We'll keep that in mind," Jesse said.

He topped his burger with ketchup, mustard, onions, relish, and hot sauce. Courtney stared at him, wide-eyed.

"You're going to eat that," she said.

Jesse smiled and took a huge bite. He chewed it contentedly.

"You just going to stare at yours," he said between bites.

She gingerly put some ketchup on her burger and took a bite. Then she took another.

"This is pretty good," she said.

"Best turkey burger in Massachusetts."

They ate in silence for a while.

"Are you watching the playoffs," Jesse said.

"What playoffs?"

"The baseball playoffs."

"Ugh."

"You mean you don't like baseball?"

"I don't like sports."

"What do you like?"

"I don't know."

"You don't know what you like?"

After a few moments, Courtney said, "I like to read."

"Read as in books?"

"Yes."

"What?"

"What do I like to read?"

"Yes."

"I like Margaret Mead."

Jesse didn't say anything.

"I like *Coming of Age in Samoa*. I mean, she was real young and she left home and went to live in a wild place and studied all kinds of different people. I think that's so cool."

"Which part?"

"All of it. She was awesome."

They finished their lunches and pushed their plates away.

"Good," Jesse asked.

"Really good," Courtney said.

Afterward, they climbed back into the cruiser and headed for the station.

Jesse stopped only once to ticket an illegally parked Mercedes. Then he got back in the cruiser.

"I love to nail a Mercedes," he said.

"Why?"

"The parking ticket is a great equalizer. Rich or poor, you gotta pay it."

"My mom says poor people don't drive Mercedes."

"Not usually, no."

"So it's a rich person who just got the ticket?"

"More than likely, yeah. Rich people hate having to pay tickets."

She thought about that for a while.

Jesse dropped her off at the station. She got out of the cruiser, then looked back at him through the open window.

"You gonna tell me why?"

"Why we had lunch?"

"Yes."

"We're going to be spending some time together over the next few months, and I thought it would benefit us both if we explored our human sides."

"What's that supposed to mean?"

"Well, I'm the police chief and you're a detainee. Technically we're on opposite sides of the law. But if we get to know each other, we might think of ourselves more as people and less as antagonists."

Courtney was quiet.

"Understanding each other will make both of us less defensive and more receptive to the other's ideas and opinions."

"You're a funny guy, you know that?"

"So I've been told. See you next week."

She watched as he drove away.

57

Rita Fiore's silver Lexus convertible was parked in front of the footbridge. Jesse got out of his cruiser and walked over to it. He found Rita sitting inside. She lowered the driver's-side window.

"Am I intruding," she said.

"Not at all."

"You're certain?"

"Completely."

"May I come in?"

"Either that or you can stay in the car and we'll keep talking to each other through the window."

Rita smiled.

She got out of the Lexus, and together they crossed the bridge.

"To what do I owe the pleasure?"

"You won't like it."

"How could I not like it," he asked as he opened the door and ushered her inside.

"Wait," she said.

Jesse removed his Colt Commander from its holster and placed it on the kitchen counter.

Rita settled herself into one of his two leather chairs. She looked around.

"Nice house."

Jesse smiled.

Mildred Memory trotted downstairs and began circling Jesse's legs, her tail twitching in the air. He reached down and rubbed her back.

"Have you any scotch," Rita said.

"I do."

"With soda?"

"Coming right up."

He prepared two drinks and brought her one.

"What won't I like," Jesse said as he sat down next to her.

"Rules first."

"What rules?"

"We're gonna play a little game called 'privileged information.'"

"Meaning?"

"We're going to protect the integrity of the defense counsel."

"How do we do that?"

"This conversation never happened."

"That bad?"

"I think so."

"Okay. It never happened. What's up?"

"Goodwin canceled our appointment and refused to set up another."

"Did he offer a reason why?"

"He did not."

"That's strange."

"There's more. Tony Devlin, my A-list investigator, tells me that the executives at state Water and Power claim not to have heard from William J. Goodwin for several years."

Jesse didn't say anything.

"Tony knows someone there, and he made a routine call in an effort to confirm who it was that rebuffed Goodwin's appeals for a rate reevaluation. His contact did some sniffing around and then informed Tony there was no record of any recent meetings between their personnel and Goodwin. The contact's research identified Goodwin as having once been actively engaged in dealings with W and P, but not for a while."

Jesse sipped his drink.

"And that's just for openers," Rita said. "Tony took a drive up here in order to have a look around. He started with Goodwin's house, which was nothing out of the ordinary. Oscar LaBrea's residence, on the other hand, was a different story. Our Mr. LaBrea lives in a two-story town house located on Osgood's Point, which Tony describes as a high-end neighborhood. He probed further and discovered that the town house is appraised for something north of a million dollars."

Jesse didn't say anything.

"Isn't this guy a meter reader?"

"Maybe he logged a lot of overtime."

"Don't kid around, Jesse. He's living in the lap of luxury."

"Okay."

"Normally we would subpoena a suspect's financial records. In order to get a peek at bank statements, investment accounts, stuff like that. But because Tony is so well connected, he was able to sniff out some information without a subpoena."

"I won't like this either, will I?"

"Mr. LaBrea is sitting on more than a million dollars' worth of top-grade investments. All purchased within the last few years."

Jesse didn't say anything.

"Odd, don't you think," Rita said.

"What about Goodwin?"

"Hard to say. He lives modestly in a house he's owned for more than a decade."

"And his finances?"

"He's made a great many contributions to water-starved countries and water-related enterprises. The accountants are going to have a field day sorting them all out. But in contrast to Mr. Goodwin, it appears that Oscar LaBrea was raiding the cookie jar for his personal enrichment. We're double- and triple-checking it, of course."

"Yikes," Jesse said.

"Exactly."

Jesse was silent for a while.

"What are you going to do," Rita said.

"I'll have a look for myself."

"I don't like this, Jesse. You'll want to be careful."

58

Jesse pulled up in front of Goodwin's modest Colonial. The small house was partially hidden behind a row of privet hedges and featured an immaculate lawn bordered by crab apple and dogwood trees, Japanese maples, hydrangeas, and a pair of stately American elm trees.

Jesse rang the bell, and after a while he heard William Goodwin's distinctive voice.

"Who is it," he said.

"It's Jesse. Please open the door."

"Go away."

"Please let me in."

"I've suffered enough."

"If you don't open the door, I'll call for backup and we'll break in."

After a moment, the door swung open.

Goodwin stood aside and motioned for Jesse to enter.

The house was furnished simply but tastefully. The main room featured overflowing floor-to-ceiling bookcases.

"What can I offer you," Goodwin said.

"Nothing, thank you."

They wandered into the living room. Goodwin was silent.

"I gather you're refusing to speak with Rita Fiore."

Goodwin looked away.

"Why?"

"I'm fearful," Goodwin said.

"Of?"

"The mess."

"What mess?"

"My mess. Oscar's mess."

"What's Oscar's mess?"

Goodwin didn't say anything.

"What's Oscar's mess," Jesse said again.

"I believe that Oscar was embezzling."

"You mean over and above what you and he had been stealing together?"

"The money that we gathered together was used for honorable purposes."

"Meaning?"

"We didn't enrich ourselves with it, if that's what you're suggesting. We used it to right a great many wrongs."

Jesse didn't say anything.

"Oscar appears to have changed the game."

"How so?"

"He stole."

"From monies which had already been stolen."

"Yes."

"For his personal enrichment."

"Yes."

"How much?"

"Excuse me?"

"How much did he steal."

After several moments, Goodwin said, "I don't really know. I only just discovered he had been doing it."

"You mean you didn't know his hand was in the till?"

"No."

"How could you not have known?"

"I was lax in my supervision."

Jesse didn't say anything.

"I was deeply involved in the larger picture. The distribution of the funds. The day-to-day I left to Oscar."

"You mean he was in charge of the proceeds."

"He handled the accounts."

"Jesus."

"That complicates things, doesn't it," Goodwin said.

"That's an understatement."

Jesse stood.

"I'll need to present this information to the district attorney," he said.

"He betrayed me. After all I did for him, the son of a bitch betrayed me."

Jesse walked to the door.

Goodwin walked with him.

When he opened it, he was instantly confronted by Oscar LaBrea, who had been waiting outside.

Oscar's nose was still bandaged, and the skin around his eyes was discolored. He was holding a Beretta automatic pistol, which he leveled at Jesse.

He pushed his way inside and closed the door behind him.

"Your gun," LaBrea said to Jesse.

Jesse removed his Colt from its holster.

"Drop it."

He dropped it, the pistol chipping a section of the polished hardwood floor as it landed.

Oscar kicked it away.

He approached Jesse and patted him down. He found the .38-caliber Smith & Wesson, which Jesse kept in his jacket. He tossed it aside.

"Fool me twice," Oscar said, a crooked grin appearing on his face.

He prodded Jesse hard in the back with the Beretta.

Jesse winced.

The three men moved toward the living room.

"Why are you talking to this bastard," LaBrea said to Goodwin.

"He knows."

"What does he know?"

"What you did."

"What I did?"

"Yes."

"What did you tell him?"

"I told him you stole."

"Why would you do a dumb thing like that?"

"I told him the truth."

"Which I suppose you thought was noble."

"I'm not going to argue with you anymore," Goodwin said.

"It's jail, isn't it," Oscar said to Jesse, waving the gun at him. "I'm going to be sent to jail. William's gonna skate and I'll get time."

"Oscar, I think you should put the gun down and act rationally," Goodwin said.

Oscar turned to him.

"Oh, you do, do you? Why did you tell him? So you could save your own skin?"

"You betrayed me, Oscar."

"I betrayed you? I was getting by on a meter reader's salary."

"That's what you were."

"Nonsense. I was your partner. I did all of the heavy lifting. But I wasn't living like you. Like this. On a commissioner's salary."

"That didn't entitle you to steal."

"It didn't? You were stealing huge amounts. The only difference is that you were handing it out like you were some kind of pasha. It was you who set the example."

"But not for myself."

"Bullshit."

Goodwin had become agitated. His voice was raised and excited.

"Bullshit?"

"You were set for life," Oscar said. "You were raking it in hand over fist and then throwing it away. Money which could have set me for life."

"You had no right to enrich yourself."

"I had every right."

"I'm through arguing with you."

"It's amazing how insensitive you are," Oscar said. "Without me, none of it would have happened."

He turned his pistol on Goodwin.

"You know what," he said. "Fuck you, William. You and your phony piety."

"Oh, please," Goodwin said.

Oscar raised his pistol and fired, hitting Goodwin in the neck. Goodwin's eyes widened. He reached for the wound, surprised to find blood spurting from it. He looked at the blood. He looked at Oscar. Then he collapsed.

As Oscar eyed Goodwin, Jesse leapt at him, hitting him in the small of his back and sending him flying.

The gun skittered away as Oscar fell forward, Jesse on top of him. He lifted Oscar's head and slammed his face into the floor. Oscar screamed.

"Fool me twice, indeed," Jesse said.

He grabbed a plastic restraint from his jacket and cuffed Oscar's hands together behind him.

He then looked at Goodwin, who continued to bleed profusely from the gunshot wound in his neck.

Goodwin raised his head and looked at Jesse, opening his mouth as if to speak. But before he could say anything, he fell backward, dead before he hit the floor.

Jesse stood. He picked up Oscar's pistol and gathered up his Colt and the Smith & Wesson.

Then he took out his cell phone and punched in the number for the station.

59

After Goodwin's body had been removed, LaBrea apprehended, and the EMTs had left the scene, Jesse was alone in the house with Captain Healy.

"It won't be pretty once the media gets wind of it," Healy said.

"It won't be," Jesse said.

"How much did he get away with," he said.

"LaBrea?"

"Yes."

"Goodwin didn't know."

"How much did Goodwin take?"

"Also unknown."

"But he felt justified."

"Totally."

"Self-righteous little bastard."

"He was, wasn't he?"

"Such an odd story," Healy said.

"A sad one."

"What about the woman, what's her name again?"

"Ida Fearnley."

"What's in store for her?"

"Loneliness. Sadness. She'll be devastated by Goodwin's death."

"But she was an accessory," Healy said.

"To his crimes, yes."

"Jail time?"

"That'll be up to a jury."

The two men headed for the door.

"You'd think it would have gotten someone's attention," Healy said.

"You'd think," Jesse said. "But he'd been in charge for decades. He was an icon. The personification of bureaucratic autonomy. Who was going to challenge him?"

"The harder they fall," Healy said.

"Exactly."

"You knew him?"

"Some. He was a strange little guy. But he made his arguments with passion and conviction. He sure got himself into my head. I can't rid myself of the image of the one and a half gallons of clean water it takes to flush away less than an ounce of piss. That's ultimately why I reached out to Rita. I thought that even if the messenger was corrupt, the message would speak loudly enough to be heard."

Healy didn't say anything.

"The only message people will hear now is the one in which still yet another public official went rogue and managed to enrich himself at the expense of the taxpayers."

"You okay," Healy said.

"Disheartened."

"Life's a bitch."

"Tell me something I don't know," Jesse said.

Jesse called Rita Fiore.

"I heard," she said, when she picked up the call. "Sounded awful."

"Sad."

"You want to tell me about it?"

Jesse swiveled his chair around so that he was facing the window.

"Goodwin rode the moral high ground to the end, which infuriated LaBrea, who assumed that because Goodwin didn't use the money for his personal enrichment and he did, he was going to be the fall guy."

"Meaning?"

"Goodwin would somehow be absolved and LaBrea would go to jail."

"Why did he do it?"

"Do what?"

"Shoot Goodwin."

"Goodwin had disavowed him. Left him dangling. They argued, but neither of them gave in. Finally he just went berserk."

"Goodwin was such a sorry man."

"But guilty as charged. Although strangely innocent at the same time."

"You can't beat yourself up over this, Jesse."

"Did you speak with Aaron," Jesse said.

"He's petitioning the court. Wants to place a lien on all of their assets."

Neither of them spoke.

"What about Ida," Jesse said at last.

"I'll still represent her."

"Because?"

"I'm not completely certain, to tell you the truth. Maybe it's a woman thing. She's definitely going to lose her job, but I sympathize with her. She barely knew what was going on. She was totally devoted to the guy and paid a steep price for it."

Jesse didn't say anything.

"I'll argue for no jail time and for her to retain her pension."

"What are the chances?"

"You have to ask that question?"

"I forgot myself."

"You did the right thing, Jesse."

"It always comes as a shock," he said.

"What does?"

"The aberrational behavior of the human race."

"Tends to get you down, doesn't it?"

"Makes you wonder why you even try."

"But somehow you manage to dust yourself off and get back into it."

"Somehow you do."

"Which is what separates you from them," Rita said.

"That doesn't make it any easier."

"No," she said. "That doesn't make it any easier."

60

Courtney was already at work when Jesse arrived.

"She showed up early," Molly said. "You're sure this is the right thing to do?"

"Can't hurt."

"She's still unrepentant."

"But a work in progress nonetheless."

Jesse found her dusting the squad room.

"You ready," he said.

"Yes."

She put the cleaning equipment away, and together they walked to the parking lot and got into Jesse's cruiser.

They headed for the downtown recreational center.

"Why are we doing this again," she said.

"Part of your community service."

"I know that. But why this?"

"I thought it might be interesting."

She didn't say anything.

They arrived at the center, parked, and went inside.

It was Family Day, and the place was packed.

Jesse was on the lookout for Pastor Charles Tompkins, who turned out to be a burly man in his late thirties, pink-skinned and balding, wearing oversized blue jeans and a heather-gray sweatshirt that read, "If You're Not the Solution to the Problem, Step Aside."

"Jesse," he said, a big grin lighting up his face.

"Pastor," Jesse said. "I want you to meet Courtney Cassidy."

"Pastor Chuck," he said as he grasped Courtney's hand. "Jesse's told me a lot about you."

Courtney looked at Jesse.

"All good," Pastor Chuck said. "All good."

He smiled.

"I'm glad you could make it on Family Day. We hold one every month. The neighborhood turns out in droves for it."

As the pastor spoke, he led them on a tour of the center.

"We offer all kinds of organized activities. Arts and crafts, computer study, exercise classes. We have a small library facility and a story time. We provide them a wholesome lunch. We keep a special eye on the children. We monitor how they interact with the other members of their family, and in this way, we come to understand the family's dynamic. If the children act out, we see it, and can try to figure out why. We're always on the lookout for families that seem troubled. When we feel it's necessary, we intervene. We've been able to provide anticipatory aid to a lot of people."

Courtney and Jesse followed Pastor Chuck as he made the rounds. People greeted him warmly as he passed. Children raced to hug him. He seemed to know everyone's name.

Pastor Chuck noticed that Courtney seemed attuned to the tension that existed in some of the families. Different from the ease and joyousness of others. These differences were palpable. He invited her to join the activities. When she agreed, he gave her an apron, introduced her to the director of food services, and asked her to assist in serving the lunch.

"I've never done anything like this before," she said to the pastor. "It makes me nervous."

"Don't worry about it. You'll do fine."

The families began to move through the service line. Courtney was put in charge of the desserts. There were three of them. Chocolate pudding, brownies, and fruit salad. She soon got caught up in the rhythm of serving, and she performed earnestly and well.

Afterward, Pastor Chuck invited her to sit with two families that turned out to be related. Each of them had three children. Only one had a male parent present.

She watched how the children all clamored for the attention of their parents.

In the family with both parents present, they each tried to give equal attention to their children.

The single-parent family didn't, and as a result, the two older children were dominant. They jousted with each other over the attentions of their lone parent, each child more demanding than the other.

The youngest child couldn't compete. She was withdrawn. She sat alone. She didn't seek attention.

Jesse noticed Courtney watching the little girl.

After a while, Courtney slid over to her and whispered in her ear.

"I'm Courtney," she said.

She offered the little girl her hand.

The little girl looked up at her. Then she took Courtney's hand and shook it emphatically. She didn't say anything.

"What's your name," Courtney said.

"Ariel," the girl whispered.

"That's a nice name."

The girl was silent.

"Who's this," Courtney said, pointing to the stuffed animal that the girl was holding tightly to her chest.

The girl relaxed a bit and showed the animal to Courtney.

"This is Arthur," she said.

"Arthur's a nice name, too."

Ariel nodded.

"May I see Arthur?"

After a while, Ariel hesitantly handed Arthur to Courtney.

Courtney made a show of shaking one of Arthur's paws. She held him up for everyone to see. The other children stopped what they were doing and watched. Then Courtney handed Arthur back to Ariel, who clutched him proudly. She was all smiles.

Courtney looked at Jesse.

He smiled at her.

Later, on their way back to the station, Jesse mentioned the incident.

"What made you do it," he said.

"Do what?"

"Talk to her."

"I understood how she felt."

"How so?"

"I know what it's like to be alone in the middle of your family."

Jesse didn't say anything.

"That's pretty intense, huh," she said.

"It is."

"I'd like to do this again."

"You mean go to Family Day."

"Yes. Pastor Chuck said it comes around once every month."

"It does."

They pulled up in front of the station. Jesse turned off the motor.

Courtney looked at him.

"This was good," she said.

Jesse didn't say anything.

"You're not so bad."

"Don't jump to any sudden conclusions."

She smiled.

She opened the door and got out of the cruiser.

Then she leaned back in through the open window.

"Thank you," she said.

He smiled.

61

Frankie Greenberg was sitting up, sipping cranberry juice through a straw, when Jesse stuck his head into her room.

"All right to come in?"

"Jesse," she said, smiling.

Jesse walked to her bedside and cautiously planted a kiss on her forehead.

"I'm not fragile, you know," she said.

"You could've fooled me."

"My dad says you've been hanging around here a lot."

Jesse pulled a chair alongside her bed and sat down. Most of the machines were gone. A lonely IV was still attached to the back of her hand.

"How are you feeling?"

"I have nothing to compare it to, but they tell me I could be feeling a whole lot worse."

"You had us going."

"That's what Dad says."

"You've got some color now."

"And I didn't before?"

"Does the expression 'pale as a ghost' mean anything to you?"

"That bad?"

"That bad."

"I still can't believe Marisol's dead. I feel awful."

"We all do. He had just a sliver of an opening, and he somehow managed to jump through it."

"You caught him?"

"Crow did."

"But not without your help."

Jesse smiled.

"I hear they're flying you home," he said.

"In the morning. Sometimes it's good to work for a big studio."

She looked at him.

"I feel that we're incomplete, Jesse," she said. "You and me. We were interrupted and now can't find our way back."

"Get well, Frankie. L.A. isn't the moon."

A tear rolled down her cheek.

"I wish I felt like I had been lucky," she said.

"You were incredibly lucky. He came within inches of killing you, too."

"Then why am I so sad?"

"Because Marisol's gone and you're not. Survivor's guilt."

They were silent for a while.

"Will I ever see you again, Jesse?"

"Of course you will," he said.

"You're not just saying that?"

"I'm not just saying that."

She leaned back into her pillows and closed her eyes. Soon she was asleep.

Before he left, he tenderly kissed her good-bye.

62

Jesse pulled into his spot in front of the footbridge. He got out of the cruiser, opened the back door, and grabbed the take-out dinner from Daisy's. Real football food. Buffalo wings, cheese fries, and a pair of chili dogs. A six-pack of Rolling Rock waited for him in the fridge.

He crossed the bridge and went into the house.

Within seconds, Mildred was at his feet.

He walked into the living room and turned on the TV. USC vs. Oregon. The game was just beginning. He had been looking forward to it all week.

He put the take-out bag in the oven to keep it warm.

He went upstairs and changed clothes, then came back down

and fed a sumptuous meal to Mildred, which she ate as if she had never eaten before.

He cracked a bottle of Rolling Rock and sat down to watch the game.

Suddenly he was aware of how tired he was. The events of the last few days had worn him down. Life in a small town was tougher than he imagined it would be.

But he had to admit that he liked it. He liked living in Paradise. More than he ever did L.A. He found himself surprisingly content. Like it was home.

Finished with her after-dinner bath, Mildred jumped onto Jesse's lap. She looked at him expectantly. He reached over and scratched her neck. Soon she was asleep.

Jesse's eyes closed, too, and when he opened them, it was the second half and the score was tied.

He kept them open for the rest of the game.

ACKNOWLEDGMENTS

Special thanks to Melanie Mintz, Joanna Miles, David Chapman, and Miles Brandman for all of their efforts on behalf of the manuscript.

Thanks to Tom Distler for his wise and generous counsel.

A tip of the hat to David Parker.

Thanks to Tom Selleck and the entire Jesse Stone film family.

My most heartfelt gratitude to Christine Pepe, whose undying quest for excellence is inspirational.

And a most appreciative nod to Helen Brann for her kind and loving support.